W9-APS-491

Jewels
and other stories

Dawn Promislow

Copyright © 2010 Dawn Promislow

Except for purposes of review, no part of this book may be reproduced in any form without prior permission of the publisher.

We acknowledge the support of the Canada Council for the Arts for our publishing program. We also acknowledge support from the Government of Ontario through the Ontario Arts Council.

 Canada Council **Conseil des Arts** **ONTARIO ARTS COUNCIL**
for the Arts **du Canada** **CONSEIL DES ARTS DE L'ONTARIO**

Cover photos by Galina Horoshman and Patty Ghillebert
Design by Peggy Stockdale

The following stories have been published previously:
"The Letter" in *Maple Tree Literary Supplement* (December 2008);
"Pool" in *Maple Tree Literary Supplement* (April 2009);
"Secret" in *Maple Tree Literary Supplement* (August 2009);
"Billy" in *Maple Tree Literary Supplement* (December 2009);
"Jewels" in *TOK: Writing the New Toronto Book 5* (April 2010).

Library and Archives Canada Cataloguing in Publication

Promislow, Dawn

Jewels and other stories / Dawn Promislow.

ISBN 978-1-894770-65-1

I. Title.

PS8631.R64J49 2010   C813'.6   C2010-904793-1

Printed and bound in Canada by Coach House Printing

TSAR Publications
P. O. Box 6996, Station A
Toronto, Ontario M5W 1X7
Canada

www.tsarbooks.com

For Rose

Contents

Pool

IS JOB WAS TO CLEAN the pool. That, and take care of the garden. Often he was called into the house to help carry the vacuum, or move a piece of furniture—man's work. They called him Ficksen. What was the name his mother had given him, though? She wondered sometimes. Ficksen. What kind of a name was that?

He lived in a room behind the house, in the servants' quarter. The room was spare and clean, like a jail cell, almost. So it struck her. It was stone, and it was white. It had a concrete floor; the bed-frame was iron. She peeped in whenever she could. Maybe Ficksen would reveal to her some essential clue about himself, in his room. But he didn't. His room remained austere—mute—as ever.

Ficksen was lean. His skin was dark, almost ebony. Sometimes she thought of him as a shadow, merely. She might see him, of a hot afternoon, slowly skimming the pool surface with the special net, the net that caught in it all the leaves, the debris that fell from the trees overhanging the water. They seemed like slow motion, his long, fluid movements.

Sometimes, turning the corner at the end of the garden, under the willow trees, she'd see him disappearing behind the pool house with a barrow of weeds, garden scissors in hand. He was part of the landscape. His clothes were navy, or a tattered tan. A camouflage.

She, watching him, had a camouflage too. A girl, supposed to be doing her homework in the cool house, in her room with its silent, reproachful desk, with her books and pencils. But she was never doing homework. She was in the garden. Where there was mystery in the dark shrubs, and behind the trees; beetles that burrowed; a life underfoot. She'd sit in the treehouse she and her brother had built. On the sturdy wooden platform, hidden in the leaves.

The pool—the pool that he cleaned—was, in the afternoons, filled with the splashing children. Home from school, in their many-coloured swimsuits, they shrieked and flashed through the water. They were her brother and sisters. She didn't swim much. She preferred playing in the shadows of the garden; being alone in the treehouse. She liked watching the shadows as they danced on the grass, on the leaves.

And she could see the pool through the trees. She watched it. It was a crystal: a pale sapphire, many faceted. It glinted in the sun.

One weekend the family went away to the country town where their grandparents lived. Ficksen was left at the house. As they drove away and she watched him waving goodbye, a dark figure at the white garage door, she wondered what he would do while they were gone. At the closed-up house, in the hot paved yard where his room was, in the still, still garden. He would have the weekend off, mostly, her mother said. He was to keep an eye on the house, feed the dogs, maybe keep the pool swept (skimming the leaves), to make the job easier on Monday. Those were his instructions.

As the car drove from the house through the leafy streets, to the highway, and out of the city, she thought about the house, with its cool, enclosing walls; about the yard, with its hot paving and the sleeping dogs; about the still garden, without her in it.

Saturday, at the house, was hot. Ficksen fed the dogs. His friend, the gardener from down the street, came over. They drank tea in the yard. They laughed a little. They sat in meditative silence. Later, his friend gone, Ficksen went down to the pool. It glinted and beckoned, as it always did, blue and cool.

He stood watching the water. How quiet it was. A dog barked in the distance; the willows rustled gently. He sat on one of the wide stone steps that led down to the pool. The steps held the sun's warmth within them. He watched the ripples in the pool, and the dragonflies that hung.

After a while he lay down on the stone, on his back, his arms folded behind his head, and fell asleep.

Later, stretching awake, he walked over to the pool chair, the green-and-white striped pool chair, and sat down on its edge. Uneasily, he sat. There was the silence around him. There was the high white wall, the dark shrubs, the hanging trees. That was all.

And then he took off his shirt. It felt so free. The breeze on his skin. He stood up suddenly and took off his shorts. He folded the shorts and shirt and laid them on the chair. On second thoughts, he took them off the chair and put them instead on the grass to the side.

He walked to the edge of the pool. Perhaps he would jump in, as he had seen the children do countless times, with their shrieks of joy. Or perhaps he would wade in, very slowly and tentatively, from the shallow end, as he'd seen the woman of the house do. Then again, there was the man of the house and the many lengths he swam, back and forth, back and forth, every morning, powerful as a fish. Which would he do? For Ficksen had never swum before, had never been in water deeper than his knees. Ficksen had grown up on a dusty farm. He had moved to Johannesburg, to the city of gold, as a young man in search of work.

Ficksen waded in, from the shallow end. That's what Ficksen did.

When the family was called by the neighbours on Saturday evening, they bundled themselves into their car, bid hasty good-byes to their grandparents, and drove the two-hour route on the busy weekend road, home. What's the matter, mommy? What's the matter? I don't know, I don't know—it's Ficksen. Ficksen? What could be with Ficksen?

Ficksen had been found late on Saturday afternoon by his friend from down the street, who'd come to see if he wanted to join him for supper. Ficksen was dead at the bottom of the swimming pool.

An image, indelible, of his ebony body in the blue, blue water. She carries it with her. And with it she carries a deep puzzlement, that no explanation from her parents, or from the world around her, ever made clear. Because he must have been puzzled too. Puzzled to discover that he wasn't laughing with glee while he swallowed water and splashed so as not to keep sinking. Puzzled to discover that the motion of the man with his arms—the churning motion—was not so easy, after all. Puzzled to discover how treacherous the glinting water was, not beautiful at all. Not cool and cooling but murderously hot, as his heart beat furiously in his chest until it burst.

Jewels

E VA HAD LIGHT BROWN SKIN that was as smooth and glossy as polished stone. Carol always wondered how skin could be so smooth—and so soft. Eva's skin smelled of soap and Nivea. Sometimes Carol put Nivea on her skin too, on her hands and arms. The smell enveloped her; became her. "Nivea Skin Cream" it said on the royal blue tin, in square white letters. The cream was thick and white.

Eva wore a uniform. She always wore a uniform. Carol had never seen her wearing anything else. Eva's uniform was blue—usually. Sometimes it was a pale blue, and sometimes—other days—it was a turquoise. Perhaps, Carol thought, she had a white one too. Whichever it was, it was crisp and clean, and freshly ironed, after being washed in the big stone sink where all the clothes were washed. It must have been dried in the sun, on the idly spinning washing line. The uniform smelled of the sun, and of the iron.

Eva wore a uniform because she was Carol's nanny. She was also Carol's brothers' nanny, and was especially in charge of the baby brother, whom she called, affectionately, Tsoko. This was a Zulu endearment, since Zulu was her language. Eva indulged Carol by speaking, fluently, in English. Carol wished she could follow her into the world of her own tongue, though. But she couldn't follow her. She had to watch her go; listen to the words carry her away. Where did they carry her, Carol wondered. To a world far away and unknown, that much was clear: rolling green hills that curved their way to the distant sea. That's what Carol thought. It was certainly not the hot, paved yard where Eva lived now, in the servants' quarter.

Eva's room was small and dark. It smelled of Lifebuoy soap, and Nivea. Her bed was elevated on strategically placed bricks: two bricks under each of the four legs of the bed. This was to keep the Tokolosh—the evil spirit—away. This is what Eva said. Carol hoped it did keep him away. She worried, though, that perhaps it didn't.

In Eva's room through the long afternoons, the radio played: voices in Zulu that rose and fell, curving their way, greenly, to that distant sea. And music, sometimes, that was filled with joy. Carol could see the flashing smiles, hear the laughter, in the music. But crackly, through the radio that was small and black, and that cowered—a creature—in the room. Carol would sit on the keep-the-Tokolosh-away bed. Carol, in her schoolgirl's uniform, her long schoolgirl legs dangling from the edge of the bed. Eva would be sitting on her chair. Her shoes hurt, she said. The shoes sat on the floor, misshapen and brown. Eva was glad to be off her feet. Carol was supposed to be doing homework, but she was never doing homework. She was in Eva's room.

On a small table (two milk crates pushed together and covered with a cloth), in pride of place, was a black-and-white photograph of Eva's three children. Her own three children. They were Angeline, Magdalene, and Godfrey. Angeline, Magdalene and Godfrey lived in Soweto with an aunt, or maybe a grandmother,

6

or some other female relative—Carol wasn't sure. She wondered about that. Who had taken the photograph, for one thing? In the picture Angeline's hair was perfectly braided, in rows. If Carol looked closely, she could see the tiny ends of the braids, the many tiny ends. Angeline had lost her two front teeth. She was seven years old. She was holding Magdalene's hand—Magdalene who was very little. Godfrey wore a white shirt with buttons: a school shirt. He was squinting in the sun. The long shadow of whoever took the photograph fell across the figure of Godfrey, and across the white wall behind him.

Carol spent much time pondering the black-and-white picture. A picture of three children she never saw, in the flesh. Angeline, Magdalene, Godfrey. Carol would repeat it to herself: Angeline, Magdalene, Godfrey. Pause. Angeline, Magdalene, Godfrey. The way Eva said it made it sound as though they were one name, not three. The names were carefully elaborate: not Angela, but Angeline; not Magda, but Magdalene. Angeline, Magdalene, Godfrey. Pause. Angeline, Magdalene, Godfrey. Carol thought of angels and God. She thought of angels she'd seen pictures of, in books. Babies with round cheeks and golden hair, and wings. Pink clouds. Angeline. She didn't know who Mary Magdalene was. Angels and God were not familiar to Carol, in her house across the yard. There was never talk or thought about angels and God in Carol's house. And they had a different religion in any case, in the house across the yard. An older—a dustier—religion, Carol thought, one taken out on special holidays, like a vase, and Carol wasn't sure about God in all that.

But Eva believed in God. She went to church on Sunday mornings. Carol would see her leaving through the white-washed back gate, wearing another uniform—the long, white robe with a blue belt that was the choir uniform. She would come home again in the afternoon, still wearing the uniform and humming softly to herself.

One night Eva sat at the kitchen table with her tea—Carol's parents out and Carol, as usual, awake past her bedtime. Carol flittered through the dark house in her nightgown, doing pirouettes. From ballet, she told Eva. Carol loved ballet. She wanted to do a perfect pirouette: that's what she really wanted to do. She spun and spun. She tossed her hair, with its long, tangled curls. Te-dum, te-dum, spinning and whirling, her white nightgown twirling, like a moth. But that night Eva was not so interested in the pirouettes. She sat quite still, her glasses lay beside her. Was she crying? She didn't move at all. What's the matter, Eva? Eva put her glasses back on. She adjusted them carefully on the bridge of her nose. She shook her head. I have so many troubles, she said. So many troubles. I don't have enough money. Angeline needs shoes. I don't know if Godfrey is going to school. I don't know. I don't know.

Carol thought Eva was talking mostly to herself. She was as if in conversation with herself. A conversation that went into air, into the empty, breathing kitchen, in the dark, still night. Because there was no one under the greenish kitchen light, in the quiet, sleeping house, to hear. Only Carol, in her white nightgown, who knew nothing at all. I don't know, said Eva. I don't know.

Carol did not know either. She did not know at all. She couldn't think what to do. She went to her room, her nightgown trailing, trailing on the tiles. There was her piggy bank. It loomed large and new in front of her—like an idea. She had no use for money. Her father gave her pocket money when he remembered. She emptied the piggy bank onto the floor, with a small clatter. There wasn't much in it: some coins, that glinted in the half-light. Crouched on the floor, in her nightgown, she counted. Thirty-five, forty, forty-five, fifty. Under her breath, she counted: fifty-five, sixty, sixty-five, seventy. She would conjure up the coins, if she could. Seventy-five, eighty, eighty-five. Coin by coin, she counted, as she crouched. Ninety-five, a hundred. There was two rand. And she gathered the coins up: they fit in the fist of one hand. The night was cool. It wasn't hot, she remembers that now. For a long time she thought the fistful was sweaty. She was sure she remembered the sweat of her palm: the clamminess, the heat, the damp coins as they rubbed. But no. She remembers now with certainty: her hand was cool and dry. And her bare feet on the floor were cool too. They moved whitely, soundlessly—like moths—along the tiles.

She came back to the kitchen and gave the two rand to Eva. Here, she said.

When Carol came home from school the next day, her mother, seated on the edge of her bed, gave her back her two rand. Eva had told her what Carol had done.

And Carol remembers, now, the silence between her mother and herself. Her mother, with her crossed legs, on the edge of the bed. There was the silence, and then the realization that came to her slowly, slowly, but with certainty, like a stain. And it was a stain. It was a taint: there forever. There were her limp hands (one filled with the useless, grimy coins). She was not powerful, as she had thought. She could not, with her limp hands, create the world in her image, after all. She could not make sure that Eva smiled her radiant smile for always, as she had wished. That night Carol buried herself under the bedclothes, in the dark of her room, and she would have stayed there forever, if she could.

Nowadays Carol lives in a different place, far away. Sometimes she watches snowflakes that fall, so soft. They fall and fall, whirl and twirl. They're like pirouettes. And if she listens (if she wants), she will hear it: a call from the other place, far away. And long ago. For Carol is no longer a girl. Despite the snow, through the muffling softness of the snow, she will hear it. Angeline, Magdalene, Godfrey. Pause. Angeline, Magdalene, Godfrey. It is a summons to her, but a summons she herself wills. A summons, a summoning. A magical summoning. Oh—if only—to summon: Angeline, Magdalene, Godfrey. Under her breath, which is a white cloud, or in the dark and private confines of her mind, she says it. And she says it—always—with a lilting Zulu intonation, an intonation that curves greenly to a distant shore, but one that is as close to her as her own. Angeline, Magdalene, Godfrey. It is an act of will, to summon, but one—she knows—that is as impotent as the frailest flower. Angeline, Magdalene, Godfrey. It's an incantation: she would wring the magic from it. Wring it and wrest it, if she could. If she could. Angeline, Magdalene, Godfrey. It's a reminder, a reproach. A wish, a prayer. The words, hard and bright, are like jewels within her. But they're also like stones.

Bottle

BELLA'S HUSBAND HAS A JOB at a hotel in the city centre. He's a security guard on the night shift. During the day he goes back to Orlando, first one bus, then another, and then a two-mile walk along a rutted road. His wages are enough to pay the rent on the two rooms, and to buy tea, bread, and jam. They drink tea in the morning, with thick slices of white bread and apricot jam. He, and the three children. The children are supposed to go to school, but often they are not at school. Bella's husband's mother, who's supposed to supervise them going to school, and who's in the house at night while they sleep, has trouble with the children. Her legs are bad, for one thing. She says she can't run after children any more. And the children are always running: running here, running there, barefoot in the dusty pathway behind the house. Their school shirts are not so white any more, and they have missing buttons that don't get replaced. Things are not so good in Orlando.

This is what Bella's husband tells Bella, when he visits her in Illovo every month. Once a month, on his day off, he travels there, on a different bus this time, and then another. He has a long, hot walk along Oxford Road, his jacket trailing behind him. When he reaches the white-walled house, half hidden behind greenery, he goes to the back gate. He knocks tentatively on the white-painted wood. He stands for a long time, then knocks again, and again. There's just the stillness of the trees. He's very thirsty now, and very tired. He pushes the gate open, latches it carefully shut behind him, and goes in. He walks straight across the paved yard, and straight to Bella's room. Bella will find him there later, fast asleep on her bed. He lies on his back, his jacket hung over her chair. She will make him tea. They will talk. About Orlando. About his mother's bad legs. About the children not going to school. About the shirts with no buttons.

Next month, Bella tells him, he won't be able to visit, because she's going away with the family. Away? They want to take the nannies this time. Where is away? They're going to the sea, to Plettenberg Bay. He's never heard of Plettenberg Bay. It's at the sea, she tells him. The sea.

He thinks that would be nice. He's heard about the sea. He knows it's far away.

Bella makes her preparations. She and Iris both will go to Plettenberg Bay, by train. They will be at the house on the beach to help the family. To cook, to clean the house. The usual. So Iris tells her.

And so it is, that while Bella's husband is doing the night shift at the hotel, and Bella's children are not going to school in Orlando, and Bella's husband's mother is moving heavily on her legs, Bella arrives at the house near the beach, in Plettenberg Bay.

In the morning she and Iris do their work. They may as well be in Johannesburg. They sweep and vacuum, they wash clothes and hang them on the line to dry. They wonder if this is all Plettenberg Bay will be, after all.

But the next afternoon the man of the house tells them he'll take them to the beach. He's found a beach where they can go. (They cannot go to the beach nearby, which is reserved for whites.) He'll drive them; perhaps they can get a ride back with one of the other nannies' employers? All the nannies go swimming there, he tells them. Swimming? Bella and Iris don't have bathing suits, but they will certainly go swimming.

And so they set off in the car. The man of the house wears no shoes here in Plettenberg Bay. Bella sees his feet, with their dark hairs, on the foot pedals of the car. There's sand everywhere on the floor of the car. She's sitting in the front, while Iris, holding the packages with their towels, sits at the back. The man wears his shirt open and untucked here too. He's in a good mood. This is what Iris says to Bella, in their language. *Esihle senhliziyo.* They laugh a little about the good mood. The car drives up a hill, away from the house, then down. They see a far-off flatness under the palest blue sky. The car speeds along a tarred road, faded to a dull black by the sun. After a while the man curses: he's missed the turn. He stops, pulls over on the side of the road. Bella hears the crickets ringing like sirens in the bush. Otherwise there's silence. The man reverses the car, frowning, and starts driving back. He finds the turn this time, next to a small, faded sign. He turns down a dirt road. The car bumps along, scuddering stones as it goes. The windows are open. The road dust gusts up behind them. Bella hears the crinkle of the plastic packets next to Iris at the back.

And then suddenly they're at the end of the road. All they can see are scrubby bushes and the pale sand dunes under a wide blue sky. That is all.

The car pulls up next to a dune. There's just stillness. Then Iris and Bella gather their packages and climb out of the car, laughing with the man about the bumpy road, about the unlikely expedition they have just shared. He starts his engine and honks the car's horn as they wave goodbye. The car drives away, its wheels crunching in the gravel.

They are two small figures, suddenly. They pick their way up an uneven pathway through the dune.

And now Bella feels a wind. Her towel, billowing, catches in the prickly scrub. She clambers up, her shoes filling with sand. And then they're there, the beach in front of them.

Bella feels the air, pure and cold. The wind whips her cheeks. Her headscarf snaps wildly behind her. And it is the light that is astonishing. She squints her eyes because the light is so white. It is dazzling. The sand is dazzling white too. And when her eyes are used to the light, Bella hears the roar in her ears. The roar of waves, the roar of the surf. And she sees the waves, how they pound and crash; advance, and recede. She sees their power. And when she's closer to the water (shoes in hand, feet wet in the sinking sand), she feels the spray blown onto her cheeks. It's ice cold, and it's salt. She can taste the rough salt on her lips.

Bella sees the other nannies, headscarves billowing. They're shrieking, shrieking with excitement. There are gulls that shriek too: grey-and-white streaks that swoop by.

Bella thinks this is the most amazing thing she's ever seen. She's standing, yes, she's standing at the edge of the sea. She remembers, now, her lessons in the dusty schoolhouse on the farm, long ago. How she sat, so still, a girl in her school uniform, her hands on the scored wooden top of her desk, listening, listening as he spoke. That was her teacher, in his buttoned white shirt, his spectacles glinting as he turned. And there's her mother, bending over the ironing board and the white shirts, in the dim light of long ago. But the schoolhouse map: with its colours (a bit faded) and its creases, spread out in front of her on the desk. There's the blue expanse that she learned was the sea.

It's the Indian Ocean, Iris. The Indian Ocean, Bella says. But Iris is not listening. Iris is laughing in the wind.

They go to the beach in the afternoons after that, when their work is done. The man drives, and drops them next to the dunes. They come back in a car with other nannies, carrying the packages, damp towels, seashells. They are laughing and wind-blown. There is sand in their toes, in their ears, in their eyes. Iris laughs as she takes off her glasses and wipes them on her apron.

On the last day, the day before they go back home, Bella goes to the beach with some empty bottles she has found. She has all sorts of bottles, with screw-top lids. Empty Coke bottles, made of thick, greenish glass, and juice bottles, of clearer glass: Bella retrieved them all. This time, driving to the beach, Bella hears a clink, clink—the bottles bumping against each other—as Iris shifts with the packages at the back of the car. And in the wind they walk more carefully, clinking, up the dune.

Together, they fill the bottles with sea water. Their skirts are tucked up, away from the waves. They submerge each bottle, and the water gurgles in with a wave. Then the wave recedes, and they wait until the next one comes. They screw the bottle tops on; the sand scrapes against glass.

The man will ask them, intrigued: Why are you taking the bottles back to Johannesburg?

We're taking the sea back, says Bella. We're taking the sea back.

The man shakes his head. He tells his wife about it later. It's a lot of trouble, carrying all those bottles of sea water, he says. And breakable, on the train. His wife is busy. She's packing the bags (the sarongs, the sandals), to go home.

The bottles make it home. Bella keeps one in her room in Johannesburg afterwards. She picks it up sometimes when she's finished her work. When she's resting in her chair. Sea sand swirls up, when she shakes it.

It's her bottle. Hers. It is, she thinks, her claim. Her claim to have been there. Her claim to have traveled the length (the breadth) of her country, over two long days. She smiles (to herself).

She tells her husband about it all, the next time he visits. She tells him about the beach. About the wind that whips, and the sand that's so white, and the sea that roars day in and day out. Day in, and day out. Bella's husband likes that part especially: day in, day out.

In the dim light of her room she shows him the bottle. He sees it: a watery dullness, contained. That is all. Bella unscrews the bottle and pours some of the water into a cup. She wants him to taste it. He holds it up: a toast. And he sips. He pulls his mouth downward. Is it a grimace? He looks at Bella. It tastes very strange, he says. Very strange.

He looks at the bottle, again. And as he watches, a shaft of afternoon sunlight comes through the window onto the grey floor, then slants up onto the small cloth-covered table, and lands gently on the bottle. The water within is lit: a momentary transformation. The water—the bottle—glows. It is golden. Bella's husband smiles. He smiles and smiles.

Somewhere

ECILE HAD A COLLECTION. On her shiny red stoep—her verandah—were the metal stands. The boy at the shop built them. He would walk over from his work and add another, when she needed one. By now the whole length of the verandah was taken up with the stands, stands of cacti. They were miniatures. Miniatures of ones that grew in the veld just beyond their town. Just where the road straightened out, and you saw you were on the open veld, no longer in the town that curved around the brown river, in the sun.

The cacti sat, each one in its own pot. There were the ones with needles, you had to be very careful with those. Often, in the beginning, she had pricked herself. Some of the needles were tiny, but they had such a capacity for injuring. A predator, a rodent in the wild, would be well kept at bay by those needles.

She had learned how to water them. Or rather, how not to water them. You could kill them with too much water. They were the opposite, she thought, of most plants, most living things. You had to be sparing in nurturing them.

Now and then, one flowered. There was no luscious abundance. Sometimes she came in the morning and found a bright red, a crimson, flower of a sudden on a green stem that had sat, barren, for months.

Cecile had roses she took care of too, a whole garden of them. They weren't nearly as intriguing as the cacti, but she cared for them nonetheless. She was dutiful with her roses. Not passionate; just dutiful.

After she had seen the cacti every morning, gone to each one and checked, Cecile could start her day. She had Annie at home to deal with, first. Annie was her maid. She lived in the Location, although she had a room at the back in the servants' quarter. Annie was supposed to take care of things: the house, the laundry. But Annie had a problem with drink and was on medication. If Annie forgot to take her pills, she became drunk and disappeared for days on end. For days on end, Cecile said.

And Cecile had her husband. He went to his shop every day, after breakfast. She couldn't reach him there, to nag him about his diabetes and the sweets he shouldn't be eating—the sweets he took out of the jars that sat on the counter in his shop.

She had two children too, but they had long ago grown up and moved away.

These were the things that she had.

She thinks about it: all that she has. She has, in fact, a large, airy house that was built for her when she was a young bride. She remembers how her husband designed it, with the architect and the builder. How she was consulted, even. Even though she didn't really know anything about houses, about what one might need in a house. A big kitchen, she said. But she didn't cook that much. Why did she need a big kitchen? Maybe she had read somewhere that women like big kitchens? Maybe.

In any case, her house had been built. It was large, and it sat on the corner of two wide streets. A corner lot was a good thing, the builder had said. It was a good thing, she supposed. The house seemed more spacious because of that. You could look out of the dining room windows and see River Street and the neighbours' white-washed porch across there; if you looked out of her bed-room window, you would see Bree Street. Another bedroom looked onto the orchard of peach trees. A little overgrown, a little sprawling, the orchard, but yielding peaches nonetheless. Her kitchen faced the paved backyard, where the washing line spun idly through the long afternoons.

Her verandah—with its polished red floor—was wide and looked onto both River Street and Bree Street. It was wide enough for her collection of cacti, while still leaving room for a couple of chairs. When her children were small they had played endlessly on the steps of the verandah—jumping, hopping, climbing. Not now, though. The grandchildren came, but not often, and they didn't play so much on verandah steps. They liked different things. They were city children. They liked going down to the river to swim. They liked clambering on rocks. No, they didn't spend much time on the verandah.

Now that she thinks about it, she should be grateful for her beautiful house. And it had been called beautiful. Visitors from the city—her relatives, her husband's relatives—were quite taken. How lovely! Your roses! And she thinks how things have changed. The relatives are no longer young: they don't come to the country for visits and picnics any more. She remembers how they liked the orchard, picking the peaches. They liked how quiet it was on River Street, too. Not like the city; that was its charm.

For her, though, she thinks she might have preferred to live in the city. Not that she had had a choice. She had married Phil, who lived in this small town. He ran the business—the store—his father had started.

She had come from Johannesburg. She was a city girl—yes! She was used to parties, shops, lots of people. She had come to visit this little town once, with a cousin. It was pretty. It had a river. That's where she and Phil had courted. On the bank of the river, as they strolled, so proper. That was 1934, things were ever so proper in those days. Not like today, of course not. He asked her to marry him, and that was that. She hadn't really thought about what it would mean. Living in the little town. Leaving the city, the parties, behind.

She remembers walking along the river, with her arm in his. She remembers how tall he was; his shock of dark hair. She leaned on his arm with her slender, slight frame. She wore a pale blue dress. She remembers the dappled leaves overhead, and the curving brown river. She said yes. That's all it took. And that was that.

And the early years of her marriage (newly installed in the house they had built) had been spent taking care of her children. In her daughter's room now there's the cupboard door that creaks when you open it. There are dresses in there, that rustle and crinkle in their tulle, that glimmer a little, she imagines, with their colours, so bright. Closed up, confined, in the dark of the cupboard. She hears them rustling, as she pushes the door shut firmly.

It was soon after her daughter left home to go to university that her husband had suggested the dress shop. He would set her up in her own shop, selling dresses for ladies. She would have something to take care of, something to mind. Minding Annie was not a full-time occupation, he had said. Minding Annie and her pills. There were the weekly bridge games and tea with the ladies, a long-standing ritual. But not enough to occupy her, even her husband saw that.

So she had got her own shop. She didn't expect to make money or anything like that, from running her shop. But then, she didn't have to worry about making money. Her husband's store made more than enough. His store, indeed, is very prosperous. Her husband knows how to do business. He does business with everyone in the town, and with farmers in the surrounding districts too. He sells lumber and steel to farmers, large pieces of equipment. He sells building materials. His warehouse is filled, floor to ceiling, with supplies of all kinds. She goes to his shop once or twice a year, and has seen for herself the booming supply centre that it is. He is a king in his domain. Talking, directing, laughing, even. Yes, he is happy there, she has seen that too.

Her shop, on the other hand, is a small project. She has one employee, Mrs van Rensburg. Mrs van Rensburg is a seamstress. She knows all about sewing, about fabrics, about buttons and ribbons. She knows about dresses. Mrs van Rensburg orders the dresses that the housewives of the town will want to buy. Dresses for church, with hats to match. Those kind of dresses. Once they had more exotic, fancy dresses—evening wear. For a few months they displayed them in the window. They didn't sell very well, though. There are not many occasions to wear evening dresses in the town. No. Ladies, in any case, prefer to travel to Johannesburg when they need a fancy dress like that. They will make a day of it. Mrs van Rensburg stopped ordering evening dresses after that.

Cecile leaves her house every morning at nine and drives to her shop. She had learned to drive specifically for this purpose. She had had a series of driving lessons with a young man some years ago. (She remembers him. His white cotton shirt; his clipboard with notes; the slow circles and circuits they did on the hot streets in the car, his voice guiding. Brake. Brake. Drive. Drive.)

The drive to her shop takes less than five minutes. She would never walk, although it has occurred to her that it might be nice. The only people she has seen walking the streets of her town are natives, who don't drive cars and have to walk everywhere, carrying their bundles, their packages. She sees children running home from school, but usually they ride their bikes, calling to each other as they wheel and loop. It would be most awkward for a woman

JEWELS AND OTHER STORIES

like her to walk along River Street. Her shoes, in any case, are not made for walking. They have little heels. And, she thinks now, it would get awfully hot in her stockings. Her slip. She sees the children's bare legs, and their flipflops. The natives have bare legs too. Sometimes they have no shoes at all. Bare legs are unthinkable for her. She will have to drive her car.

She drives very slowly. She's not confident, even though she's been doing this route for years. The streets are quiet. There are no cars on River Street; hers is the only one. In the hot midday sun she drives home again for lunch; her husband joins her from his shop across the street.

This morning she's getting ready to leave. She smoothes her skirt. Annie is busy with the breakfast dishes in the soapy sink. There's the clunk, clunk, of the dishes; the gurgle of water as Annie empties the sink. The washing line across the yard twirls idly in the sun. Cecile watches it, as it turns. Soon it will be hung with the white sheets. And Annie will be snoozing on her chair, in the narrow shadow against the wall. Cecile feels a twinge of impatience. That backyard: its stillness, its silence. She's had enough of it.

She has an idea. She will take the car but not go to her shop. She will do something different.

She's never done this before. She never takes the car anywhere, apart from her shop. Sometimes on a Sunday afternoon they go for a drive, she and her husband. He drives, then, down to the river, and they sit in the parked car, and watch the willow trees trailing over the brown river, and the children whooping and clambering on the bank. Sometimes they get an ice cream and sit on the bench outside the ice cream stand while they eat.

And once or twice a year, Piet from her husband's shop drives her and her husband all the way to Johannesburg to visit her son and daughter-in-law. She sits in the back, while her husband sits up front and banters with Piet. They talk about the shop. On and on, about numbers, about quantities. Tonnes of timber; truckloads of steel. They laugh sometimes. Cecile watches the veld go by outside the window. It's dusty and brown.

In Johannesburg, in the leafy suburbs where her son lives, she sits and listens to the children shouting in the garden, in the pool. She pretends attentiveness to her daughter-in-law, who is busy. Busy with the children, organizing her household, the maids, the meals, the kitchens. Cecile sits quietly under a tree. Sometimes she works on her crocheting, which she carries in her bag with the tortoise-shell handle. She brings peaches from her orchard. The children eat them greedily, juice dripping onto their shirts.

But today, standing at the kitchen window and imagining the white sheets and the paved backyard—Annie asleep on her chair— she has decided to take the car somewhere. Somewhere completely different. She cannot walk in her town, but she can drive.

She calls Mrs van Rensburg and tells her she'll be in late today.

She feels a little shaky as she climbs behind the wheel of her car. She reverses out of the driveway in her usual cautious way. There are no other cars on the street. The traffic light on the corner is red, and she stops, then drives.

She sees, as though from a great distance, her shop go by on her right. It seems to be gliding, but of course it's she who's gliding by. "Your Dress Shop" is written in loopy white script on the window. She catches a glimpse of Mrs van Rensburg's thick figure, the glint of her spectacles, behind the glass.

And she's at the end of the street, which is the main one, and at another traffic light. She turns right, and is on the road out of town. She has never been here on her own. She may as well be eloping—well, that's the wrong word, of course. But still. She is passing, now, the Location. Where Annie lives. There are the sprawling tin shanties glinting in the morning sun. And then she's on the open road.

Her car is motoring along quite smoothly. She, in her stockings and heels, she feels quite cool, not hot at all. Actually, she has a feeling of lightness, of taking flight. As if she were in an airplane. She's been in one of those. She and her husband went to Europe once. A six-week trip, flying from capital to capital. It stands out in her mind as an enchanted, twirling time. But long ago and far away. Enclosed and sealed off, in memory.

Now, two miles out of town, in her yellow Peugeot and her stockings and heels, she has a feeling of flight. She could go anywhere. Couldn't she? Perhaps she should keep driving and see where she ends up. She doesn't know the way to any particular town, the dusty towns that she's passed through on the way to Johannesburg with her husband. There's a turn-off somewhere here, to Bloemfontein. She could take that, couldn't she?

She feels as though a great weight is off her chest. She's not sure what that great weight could have been, exactly, but she feels it's lifted all the same. She has cast off her town. Cast off! There's no River Street here, no neighbours' white-washed porch across the way. There are no ladies playing bridge, no bone china cups. There's no Mrs van Rensburg with her spectacles and dresses. Her house—her house—is gone too. She sees just the horizon now. It shimmers, a little. The earth is reddish; just a few scrubby bushes here and there. That is all.

She sees a turn-off in the road coming up. She signals long in advance to the lone car behind her. She takes the turn. She sees a farm up ahead. There's a house; some corrugated iron shacks at the back; chickens in the yard.

She goes past the farm, motoring smoothly. She sees the farmhouse and its red roof receding in her mirror. It gets smaller and smaller. Soon it is a distant speck. And she drives on.

And now there are no familiar landmarks; no landmarks at all. There's a tree coming towards her. It is bare of leaves. A sentinel. She feels unmoored, suddenly. She has gone far enough. She feels a little breathless, as though she has been running a great distance. She decides to pull over.

She parks her car on the side of the road and sits for a long time. She watches the horizon, and the pale sky. She closes her eyes, leans her head against the window. After a while she falls asleep. Her sleep is drenched, and dreamless. She wakes suddenly. There's a fly buzzing against the window: back and forth, back and forth it goes.

The sun is high in the sky. It's beating down. She has to squint to read the time on her wristwatch. It's almost eleven.

With a start she remembers her dining room, and the table set for two. She sees the dining room in her mind's eye: cool and silent, with its sideboard of dark wood, and the silver samovar glinting in the half-light.

She sits up and straightens her skirt, her blouse. She starts the engine and checks her rearview mirror.

She turns, reversing the car. She can't believe what she's done. She has left her town, in her car, by herself. She has been on a road to somewhere else. She can do it. Tomorrow she will do it again. And the day after that too. She will go to Bloemfontein tomorrow. Who knows what she will find there, what she will do. She can do whatever she likes in Bloemfontein, because no one knows her there. Maybe at the river she can take off her stockings, put her feet in the water? She feels breathless at the thought of it.

She drives a little faster now than she's ever done before, on the road back to her town. She gets home just before her husband does, for lunch. Did you have a good morning, he says. Oh, yes, the usual, she says. With Mrs van Rensburg—you know.

She goes onto her verandah, after lunch. There's one of the cacti that she's had her eye on for months. It was doing poorly. Today, now, it has bloomed. There's an orange flower. The deepest, richest colour.

River

THE RIVER JOURNEYED ITS WAY across plains of scrub. It was low in the long, dry months, but when the rains came it was full to raging. It flooded, then, overflowing the banks in its power. But in the little town where her grandparents lived, the river slowed down. There were trees along the banks that bent over the brown current as it passed. The river coiled lazily around bends there, like a snake.

After lunch on Sundays they would go down to the river and walk along its rough, uneven bank. They clambered on the grey and brown and black rocks, and crossed the swaying suspension bridge over the wide part of the river. There was giant Flat Rock, which sloped gently into the river. On Sunday afternoons people would lie on the rock and sunbathe, faces up to the sun. She did this, too. She felt the rock beneath her back. It held the sun's warmth within it. It was part of a unity: sun, rock, river, sky. For a moment—when she lay there on the rock—she was part of it, part of the unity.

One day it was suggested they go swimming. They had seen the local children splashing near the bank, yelling and calling as they played. They swam in some eddying pools where the river was trapped between rocks.

She and her brother, sun-brown in their swimsuits, healthy and strong. He was younger than her; he followed her and copied her. Go away, she said, go away from me! But he wouldn't go away. He followed her, his face earnest and determined. He was chubby, and his stomach jiggled when he ran. Fatty! she called after him. Fatty! He followed her, devoted as ever. They were waiting for the car. They stood in their flipflops on the steps, together.

Their uncle would take them swimming. Their mother would stay at the house. She was reading her book, lying on the blanket outside. The lizards baked on the rocks nearby. Or they rustled, sharply, in the stones.

Their father was going for a drive to see the property. There was land he had, a farm, and brown veld that stretched to the sky. She had seen it once. From the steps, she watched her father reverse out of the driveway. Then the car drove away, up the street. She heard the engine becoming faint. And then she couldn't hear it at all. The street lay empty in the sun.

The old people—the grandparents—were napping. Family lore had it that their grandfather had been a powerful swimmer in his youth. He had saved a boy once from drowning. He wore a ring on his finger to this day, engraved, a gift from the family of the rescued boy. She tried to imagine it: her grandfather swimming in the river. She couldn't. He was tall and strong, she could see that. But these days he spent Sunday afternoons with the radio at his ear, listening to rugby. The game was on far away, at the stadium in Johannesburg. She could hear it: the broadcaster's voice shouting, mounting with excitement, the radio crackling with it, and the roar, the spectators roaring as one. And it was a roar. Like a great, many-headed lion, dun-maned, roaring out of the little black radio—but dimly—at her grandfather's ear. He wore long pants and a shirt unbuttoned at his neck. His pale hands fiddled with his pipe.

Their uncle was ready. He was young. He got bored at the house. He would take the kids swimming, yes.

They climbed into the car. She sat in front; her brother, at the back. Her uncle honked as they drove away down the street. Perfect day for swimming, he said. She held her towel on her lap. She could see her mother's white arm waving, waving at the gate.

At the river her uncle parked on the side of the road. They could see the brown stream, smooth and curving like a ribbon, through the trees. They clambered out and went into the water at the eddying rock pools. They joined the other children splashing. Their uncle sat on the rock and watched them. Then he lay down, flat on his back. The children laughed. Come in with us, come in, she called. He got up and stretched. He'd come in. He ventured in slowly. She watched him. She saw his legs below his bathing suit, with their dark hairs. And then, with a splash, the droplets scattering like shards, he was in with them.

Can we go out a bit, she said. Outside of the shallows, she meant. It was too easy in the rock pools, no challenge for them. The thrill of it; the risk of it. Can we go out?

So they swam out into the brown river. The two children; and their uncle. She could feel the muddy bottom sucking at her feet. She kicked, and freed herself. She was adrift. And then the three of them were floating free, paddling on the river. This was nothing like the crystal blue pool that they swam in every day at home. The girl saw her brother's brown face bobbing behind her, and his glistening dark hair. She saw her uncle's paler face and his clear hazel eyes.

She was confident in water, she had trophies at home for swimming. She liked showing off, too. To her uncle; to her brother. They followed her now.

She was a cork, buoyant and light, bobbing along. Her brother laughed as he bobbed. She saw his cheeks, brown and full.

But the river surprised her. It was wide, now she saw. Its current pulled her, stronger, much stronger than her, after all. It was insistent, the current; it wanted her that way, that way, where it was going on its way. It carried her along. Not her way. Not her way at all.

She saw now that the three of them, the three bobbing heads, had been pulled quite a way along the stream. She couldn't see Flat Rock any more, or their brightly coloured towels. The bank now was not the familiar one, the one next to the rock. The splashes and shouts of the children in the shallows were now just distant, thin sounds. She heard her uncle calling her across the rolling stretch of water between them. Not loud. Very low. Loud would be panic. Come back now, come back. And she saw his face above the brown water, and his hazel eyes. She saw her brother's face too now, with its look of puzzlement; a question. There was a rock coming towards her; she pulled herself there.

It was a long time, after she had clung to that rock, and her brother to another, her uncle to a third, before they slowly pulled themselves, or rather, her uncle pulled her, and then her brother, to the bank. To the solid bank with its rough stones. The rocks and trees spun as she stood. She remembers the dizziness, the dizziness she felt. Her brother shook himself dry, like a dog. She saw his plump legs, and the beads of bright water shatter. He had a scratch. There was a thin trail of blood down his leg. He started to cry.

They made their way back to their towels, to the car, her brother's towel trailing behind him on the rough ground: red, orange, and blue, like a tattered flag. Her uncle's bare feet picked their way over the stones. And there was she.

When they got back to the house, they clamoured to tell their parents, their grandparents, about their afternoon. Their adventure—their mishap—recreated in the telling. They laughed. They jumped and interrupted each other. We had to swim like crazy, they said, like crazy. They were heroes. They had prevailed. That was the story, the story they told.

In her telling, though, she didn't say about the brownness of the river, how she couldn't see the bottom, and its bigness, and its wideness, how she couldn't see the bank. How it pulled with all its strength, and would have carried her away. And she didn't say about the fear in her uncle's hazel eyes and—especially—about her brother's chubby face and his glistening, dark head. She didn't say about the sun no longer warm, that flashed, like an attack, and about the panic in her chest that was a wildly fluttering thing. She didn't say about how she clung, wordless, truly wordless, for once.

She had looked down the river, to where the river was going. To the bend at the trees where the water went on its way. You couldn't see it after that, the river. It went away, there. Away. She didn't say about that.

Billy

I WAS BORN IN THE YEAR 1969 in a room with a sand floor and corrugated iron walls. My mother told me I tumbled out of her, crying and bloody, with the help of her mother, my grandmother. My mother was eighteen years old.

The sand floor I remember, because when I was older I used to sit on the sand, and draw lines in it with a stick. Sometimes I would draw the shape of a cow—the cow who had stopped giving milk one day, and died. Other times I would draw a circle, shaped like the sun that beat down on us all day, and dried up all the water in the stream that flowed nearby. Other times I drew my mother's face. She had a skin smooth as the rounded stone that I kept in my pocket. I had found the stone while playing in the dried-up stream bed. But I never drew my mother's face with a smile. Sometimes my mother had tears trickling slowly down her cheeks. Her tears, though, didn't come so much any more—they had dried up, too.

I remember the tin walls of our house, because they creaked and sighed in the heat. Sometimes you couldn't touch them, they were so hot from the sun. Once, the big rains came, which we had waited for, for so long. The rain beat on the tin walls like a drum and I was afraid and I was crying, while my mother held me to her chest. The tin walls leaked too, that time. Water gushed through the sides, until the sand floor was wet and muddy. My mother laughed, because she was so happy the rains had come at last.

At night I lay next to my mother under our blanket. My mother's body was thin as a bird's. She had fed me milk from her breasts when I was born, but that milk had dried up too. I heard her telling my grandmother that, many times. I have no milk, I have no milk, she said. Her tears would fall when she told my grandmother that.

But under our blanket, my mother would tell me stories. Stories about her, and about our tribe, which was all broken now, about the relocation, and about me. Her stories, unlike the stream and her milk, never dried up. They flowed always in her, as fluid and abundant as the most fertile river.

She told me about the rolling green hills where she was born. How there was water flowing there in the rivers and streams. How the cows were fat, and their udders filled with milk. She sang me songs from that time, that would send me to sleep.

During the long, hot days, my mother and grandmother would sit on the ground outside. Sometimes they turned our tin buckets over and sat on those. My grandmother would gather sticks for a fire—clambering in the stream bed—while my mother sat, often, doing nothing at all. She would be watching the distant horizon, which moved, I thought, in the heat. I would sit in the sand drawing shapes with my stick. Sometimes I would chase the scrawny chicken that pecked in our yard. She didn't care much— the chicken—anyway.

One day my father came. He came walking along the dust road that led from the horizon. He was a tall man and he walked slowly because he was tired, and he had come very far. He worked in the white man's city, far away, my mother told me, so that he could send us money for food. But not much money came mostly, and there was not much food.

On the day after my father came, my mother got me ready. She whispered in my ear, be good, boy, be good. You will come back soon. I was to go back with him to the white man's place where he worked. With a laugh, he put me up on his shoulders. I was high up, above everything. The scrawny chicken pecked away far below. I saw my grandmother's face, upturned, her skin folded and wrinkled like an old sack. She was smiling at me, happy that I was to go somewhere, somewhere with my father, my father strong and good.

We set off along the dusty road, my father and I, with me on his shoulders. We walked many hours this way, until we reached another road—a tarred road this time, not a dirt road any more. There were cars on this road that roared by now and then.

At a place next to the road we stood for a long time, waiting for the bus. I was very tired and sat down on the dirt at my father's feet. But my father had to stay standing, in case the bus came in a roar and didn't see him. When the bus came, and my father picked me up, I could feel his rough shirt on my cheek.

My father had with him a flask of water. He didn't drink any though, he only gave sips to me. He had a dry piece of bread my mother had wrapped in one of her cloths, but I couldn't eat that. I didn't eat much, in those days. My stomach was very small and not strong, and not used to much food.

I don't remember the rest of the journey, but I know there was a train that took us to Johannesburg. I remember waking up in a small dark room that did not have tin walls. There was no creaking sound of the tin in the sun, and I didn't hear the chicken scrabbling in the dust, as I did when I woke up in the mornings at home. My father was sitting in a chair looking at me. He was smiling, a little.

Come, they want to meet you. Come, come, he said.

Later I sat on a chair at a table, and there were many voices around me, and the large white faces of children with brown hair. They were smiling and laughing, these children. They touched me, even. Billy, they said. Billy! They laughed and laughed. They spoke many words in a tongue I had never heard. My father explained to me, your name here, in Johannesburg, is Billy. Billy. Do you see? He laughed too. I didn't laugh. I had a name already, a name my mother had given me. My father told me he had a new name in Johannesburg too, not his old name any more. That's how it worked with names in Johannesburg, he said.

In the mornings, when the children went to school, I would sit in the kitchen while Lena, the cook, and my father drank tea and ate their bread. Lena spoke our language too, so I could understand them talking, this time. They tried to make me eat, but my stomach was still hard and tight, and I couldn't eat much.

In the afternoons, the children came home, and I would hear them calling Billy, Billy, through the house. I had been waiting for them, sitting at the kitchen table while Lena worked. I went with the children, and we played. We played chasing games, like I used to try and play with the chicken at home. But I didn't have a stick to draw shapes in the sand with, and I missed that. And there was no sand there, in any case, at the house in Johannesburg. There was green grass only, and many, many trees. There was a bright blue pool of water that I kept far away from, out of fear. The children laughed when I hid behind the trees, away from the water.

I missed my mother and her stories at night. At night in Johannesburg I watched my father's cigarette glow red in the dark, in his room. I listened to his radio which had voices that rose and fell, from far away. Sometimes they were arguing, the voices, and sometimes they were laughing. And sometimes they were talking about things I had never heard of.

After many weeks the time came for my father to take me back home. We travelled the same long journey, but going the other way this time. We had soft, fresh bread with us, wrapped in shiny paper, and the bread was filled with things I had learned to eat, at the house in Johannesburg. I had milk to drink, too, in a plastic jug with a lid. My stomach did not feel so tight and hard any more like it did before.

My father carried many heavy packages on our journey home. He had to stop every while and put the packages down to rest his arms. The packages were filled with things for my mother to cook on our fire: maize flour and rice. My mother—running towards us—cried many tears when she saw me and my father and the packages coming along the brown, dusty road. But those were tears of happiness.

The day after my father had brought me and the packages, he went back again to his work in Johannesburg. After that, other packages of flour came for us every month. My mother and I would walk along the road and travel the long bus ride to the post office near the train station, to pick the packages up. They were wrapped in brown paper and sometimes they had string tied around them to keep everything tightly inside. We would take them, and carry them home with us, to the house and to my grandmother. My grandmother would always be waiting for the packages, her face creased into smiles.

I had some schooling at the house behind the post office. It wasn't too much schooling. It was very far, the school, and some days my mother was too tired to take me on the long walk and the bus ride. Other days we would get there and the school was closed. The teacher himself couldn't get there on those days. That's what my mother told me. We would sit on the wooden doorstep, then, and rest in the sun before setting off home again. I would stand on a crate and look in the schoolhouse window. I'd see the black-board, dusty with chalk. There were yesterday's lessons on the board. I would read the lessons through the window. And then I would read them again. I saw the wooden tables in a row. The row wasn't straight and sometimes a chair was overturned. I yearned to straighten the chair, to sit in it. A line of sunlight fell across the tables. The line moved, so slowly, as I watched.

It is 1995 now. You know that of course. My mother died last year. We buried her in the dry earth where she lived most of her life. It is strange, but there was a beating pouring rain on the day we carried the wooden box to the hole in the ground to bury her. The brown water ran and gushed in the furrows, and our spades dug into brown mud as we filled her grave.

She used to say—shaking her head—that it was a wonder I had grown up, after all. A wonder, she said. And she'd shake her head. My father would joke that it was the packages of maize flour at the post office in Bethal that did it. She would laugh a little when he said that. But then she would reprimand my father, with a click of her tongue, for making jokes. It's not a matter for jokes, she said.

I live nowadays with my girlfriend in a flat in Jo'burg. She calls me Makandiso—as you do—which is the name my mother gave me when I was born. I do my work in a room of my own in our flat. The room has a wide window. I can look out and see the pale sky. I start working soon after my girlfriend has gone off to her job, after we embrace and I smell her fragrance, and feel her soft skin against mine. I drink my tea, and I look out of my window, at the morning sun that comes as surely as anything. I have my easel that waits, with a canvas quite blank. I gather my materials, and I start.

I have a real pencil now, not a stick anymore. And I draw on paper, or on canvas, not on sand anymore. I draw all sorts of things. I draw the stories my mother told me, when she sang me to sleep in our house. I draw pictures of wide, rolling plains, and hills covered with long grass. I draw huts in a circle, and cooking fires, and the lowing cows. I draw songs, also, and laughter and smiles. But I draw darkness, too, our tin house on the farm. My mother's face with no smile, her mouth a straight line.

And I draw the present, where I live now. I draw in colours, many colours. I draw many people's faces—the faces of people in the great city where I live. It is my city—our city—now. But you know that too.

Just a Job

I'LL TELL YOU WHAT HAPPENED before I came here. My job before this one. I worked for a family in Athol. It's the best job I had.

I remember the day I got the job. I was walking, walking all day, up and down the streets. I was hot already and tired and I was thinking maybe I have to go back now, back to where I was staying in Alexandra with my sister. No job on any of those streets, in any of those houses, nothing. Then I saw the house. The last house on the street. It is a white house, but covered with lots of green creepers. And lots of shade. I was thinking it looks pretty, maybe it's my lucky one. There is a long driveway. I was worried because I was looking for the back door, the servants' quarter, and I was walking on the main path, and I could only see the front door. A big wooden door. But then I found the back door and I saw Emily and she called the madam. And then I waited and waited. I was waiting the whole day at all the back doors. I was tired and I sat there on the step at the back waiting.

Then the madam came and I thought to myself right away I like this lady. She wasn't so sharp like the other ones—how they are—with the sharp voices. I think she was busy just before I came because she had a look like she was busy and her hair was falling from her pony tail. And she didn't ask me so many questions like the other employers: Can you polish silver, do you do good ironing, references this, references that. No. This madam she ask no questions. Hello Esther, she says, when I tell her my name. Is your pass in order, she says. Yes, ma'am, I told her, yes ma'am, everything in order with the pass book. OK, she says, Emily will show you everything. And that's that, she give me the job.

Then Emily took me in the kitchen and gave me bread and tea because I was very tired from the day of walking and I still had to go the long way back to Alexandra to sleep. Emily I like right away. Emily's children were also living in Alexandra, same as my children—her husband worked at a parking garage in town. My husband—he was still my husband then—he was working in Pietersburg. But already that time, I hardly saw him, we were not really married any more. Sometimes he sent money for the children, and sometimes there was no money. That was my husband, how it was.

So the next day I started my job there. I came with my bag, and Emily showed me everything and my room which was next to hers, and Josias's room on the other side. Josias I see he is a very quiet man. He hardly speaks English. I think he's newly come from the Transkei. I think the madam just leaves him to do his work in the garden, and with the pool. This madam is not so fussy, with the garden. One other madam I had was always telling, telling the garden boy, about the garden: the flowers something this, something that, the weeds here and the weeds there. I don't know about gardens, but this house I see it's not the kind of garden I've seen before, all the rows of flowers like that. No. This one has weeds—even I can see they are weeds. Josias busy, busy with the wheelbarrow, but often I see Josias on his chair at the back smoking his cigarette. The madam don't mind. I see this. And this pool—this pool is a pool that's got trees bending all the way over it, like it's a river near the farms, and the trees all the time dropping leaves in the pool. And even I see the children in the pool with the leaves—and Josias cleaning the pool—but still there's lots of leaves. This madam—I don't think she noticed so much the leaves.

Me, I like this garden. I don't know about gardens, but this one even me I think it's beautiful. It has much shade—even places you can't see. Those children even hiding there sometimes in the garden, you can't find them. And the madam calling and calling, and even me calling and calling—and no children. They hiding down there behind the trees.

And then there was dogs in that house. Two big dogs. And these dogs I see Josias in charge of them. Josias supposed to feed them every night and give water in their bowls and this, but I see those water bowls dirty at the back of the yard, and those dogs mostly sleeping there while Josias smoke his cigarette in his chair. This all I see.

And the madam, you can't see that madam. I was used to madams standing in the kitchens there talking, talking—telling me everything. And showing me the dusting and this and that. This one I say—nowhere. Where is she? I don't know where is she.

In the afternoons the children come home from school. Three children. They just children, busy, busy with themselves. They fighting also sometimes and Emily shouting at them behave.

And at night the master come home. I like him also. He's a happy man. He's laughing with the children. He says hello Esther to me, and he smile friendly. He kisses his wife. I think he loves his wife. Why do I say this? I don't know, I just think so. First of all, his wife—the madam—she very beautiful. She have very smooth skin. And also, she very quiet lady. She not talking, talking. I think the master, he likes that.

After the first day I see the madam has a studio in the garden where she is always. She paints pictures. I see the pictures. These pictures I don't like so much—they just colours. Lots of colours. But the colours I like I suppose. One time I see she painted a flower— but it's not like a flower. I only went two times in that studio of hers, because she doesn't want to be disturbed in that studio. She's a lady doesn't want to be disturbed. That's what Emily told me.

So I was busy, busy in that house, cleaning every day, but I'm very happy that no one is behind me telling me the beds not straight here, not straight there. Me and Emily used to talk about Alexandra, what's going on there. Because after that her husband came one time and he was telling her news of her children, and so her husband now sometimes had information about my children also. And her husband sometimes taking things if I have to send for my children: Old clothes the madam gives me, from *her* children, and I buy sugar at the grocer on the corner, and send it home to Alexandra.

But my job is the laundry, and I have to wash and iron the master's shirts. He got a cupboard full of shirts—mostly white ones, but some with stripes, and blue. And he has a row of ties in all colours, and all his suits lined up in the cupboard. And he very particular about his shirts. He like his shirts. Josias is the one who polishes his shoes. Josias always polishing, polishing the shoes at the back door.

And the master kind man. One time he had to go to the police station and pay thirty rand so Emily's husband can come out. And even other times that happened, because Emily's husband always had trouble with his pass. And sometimes he took Emily's husband in his car to the bus for Alexandra, because it was far for Emily's husband to walk. He got kind heart. He also joking a lot. He always joking in the kitchen with me and Emily. Even Josias, he tries to talk and joke with Josias, but Josias is not the talking kind I told you. And Josias is not understanding in any case the English.

And that master he works very hard also. He leaves the house every morning at seven. Emily supposed to squeeze his orange juice and make his toast at fifteen minutes before seven already. And then he's gone. And he only comes home near seven again, in time for dinner. He carries his briefcase, I see him. He look a bit tired, but he still smiling and polite even to me.

And those children—well they messy, like all children, and I was tired sometimes of picking up everything from the floor. The boy—he had a temper that one—but he's a good boy also. I like those children. The only time I don't like working in that house is when the master and madam go overseas, and the madam's parents come to stay in the house with the children. Six weeks we had with them. Oh, me and Emily worn out when we finished with that. Even Josias I think had enough because the old man is telling him there's too many leaves every day in the pool, and he must be sweeping the patio. And this and that. And that old lady, everything must be perfect in the house. The house is so clean—me and Emily laughing about that. The children also not used to so strict. I think they happy when their parents come home. And they bring a suitcase of presents for everybody. They brought me a scarf, and one for Emily.

But one day me and Emily noticing some different things. First of all the madam is looking even less around her in the house. She's more quiet than usual. She just walking through the kitchen, even forgetting sometimes to say good morning Esther, like she used to.

It's one Sunday the family having lunch on the patio. Emily was off, she went to church. I had to clean up after lunch. I'm sitting in the kitchen waiting for them to finish when the master he come into the kitchen and say sorry, Esther, there was an accident at the table. Sorry about the mess. We finished now. I go and I see the tablecloth (it's one of the ones that come from overseas with lots of colours also). The tablecloth is half pulled off the table, it's in a heap on the floor, and many glasses and plates are broken on the floor, and everything is spilled. And everyone gone from the table. I don't know what happen, I never seen anything like this before. But I think what happen is the madam she pull the tablecloth off the table, while they all sitting there. I think the madam angry, but that madam she never raise her voice, so I think she so angry she just pull the tablecloth off. That is what I think.

Nobody say nothing after that about it. The children say nothing. Everyone gone to their own business in the house. The madam she go in her studio, the master he go in his bedroom, the children later I see swimming in the pool. Why's the madam angry? I don't know. In that house you hear nothing—nobody shouting ever, nothing. My husband, if I'm angry, I shout and tell him. And he shouting also. But in this house, no. And the master joking again later in the evening, in the kitchen, when Emily is back from church. But I see he not looking the same. And me, I'm not wanting to joke this time.

After that I see the madam she not in her studio so much. Sometimes she stay in her room in the afternoons. She tell me she's resting. But she was never resting before. And sometimes in the morning she goes out in her car, and she comes again long past lunchtime, but she never used to be doing that before. And sometimes two days go by and she's not in her studio.

And the children—she's not paying them so much attention after that. She used to be sitting eating breakfast with them, before they go to school—but those days she still in her room that time, and then the children go to school and they calling bye mom, bye mom, and she calls bye from her room. And Emily takes her tea in the morning, and Emily say the madam she's lying in her bed still.

Then even I'm feeling a bit uncomfortable with that, because I would like to help the madam but I don't know what to say. And me and Emily don't even know what's the matter.

And every night the master comes home and he goes and change out of his suit and then he come for dinner, and Emily's the one who serves the dinner and Emily tell me the children talking, talking at the table, but the madam not talking, and the master he talking to the children and he joking but Emily thinks it's not his old joking, like it was before.

And sometimes I see the master after dinner he go straight to his study and shut the door, and in the morning I see all his papers and files on the desk in the study, because I think he's doing his work there. But before that he used to sit on the patio with the madam after dinner, and Emily used to bring them coffee from the special coffee machine that he likes that he brought from overseas. But even I notice he doesn't use that coffee machine any more, even on Sunday morning like he used to.

And the children still talking and playing all day, but now they getting more naughty. And me and Emily have to shout at them because they not listening and the madam is not there, she's in her room only, not paying attention. And the boy I not sure he's doing his homework so much those days because he always fighting with his sister, or he's following Josias when he's cleaning the pool, and even Josias I think is noticing that everyone is feeling uncomfortable in that house now.

But I happy to see that the master goes the same early to work, and he's wearing his shirt that I take care of so good, because in truth I like that master, I like that man.

And then one day out of the blue I come in the kitchen in the morning and Emily is very upset. She tells me the master gone this morning to work but he took a suitcase with him, and he told Emily, take care of the house Emily, and the children, and the madam, Emily. And me and Emily go later when the madam's out to their room and I see many suits are gone from his cupboard, and there's a big space in the cupboard where his shirts and ties were, and me and Emily standing there and looking and looking.

And for two weeks after that the madam and the children alone in the house, but the madam says nothing to us, and I hear the children say their father he's "on business," and sometimes now we hear the madam on the phone talking, talking to some people. To her mother, to some other people, some lawyers, we don't know.

And then one day the madam tells me the master is fetching me in the car tonight because his new flat where he lives needs cleaning, and then she say about getting divorced and she was crying a lot but still she didn't explain why they getting divorced. And then she go again in her room and close the door.

And that night the master come for me in the car and we drive to his new flat which had one bedroom and a living room and kitchen. All he had in the flat was his shirts and suits and ties and shoes, and I noticed the shoes needed polishing. He also had all his papers and his briefcase on a table, the way he used to have it in his study. I told him he needed Josias to polish his shoes and he laughed then. He said his shirts were going now to the dry cleaners, but I told him they don't starch them so good as I do, at the dry cleaners. He was laughing then too.

And I cleaned out the cupboards properly in his flat, and he told me this flat is "serviced" so people come and clean it every week. But the service people don't clean inside the cupboards, that's why I had to come. And this flat is in a building with a lift and there's a man for security at the front, and I think it is an expensive flat, but I was thinking of the garden with many trees and even the weeds which were beautiful, that the master couldn't see when he was here in this flat. Because when I looked out of the window of the flat all I could see was the parking lot full of cars.

And soon after that the madam told me and Emily and Josias we have to find other jobs because they selling the house. That's how come I work here now.

I wonder some days where they are now. If the master is still in that flat next to the parking lot. The madam told me she and the children are moving to a smaller house, and she can't afford three staff any more. She told me the master very good man, he gives her enough money, but she doesn't want to waste, that's what she told me. I don't have her phone number or the address where they went. I stayed in Alexandra with my children before I found this job and started to work again. Emily works not far away, at another house, and Josias I don't know where he went. I know it was only a job, but when I think about us: the madam, the master, the three children, me, Emily, and Josias, I think I would like to stay like that, just like it was, in that house.

I know where that flat is, where the master is. Sometimes I have an idea I could go there on my day off, on the bus. It would be late, after seven o'clock, because he's at work I know before that. I think I would like to make the master a cup of tea in that small kitchen of his, and serve it to him. But then I think I would like to get myself a cup, and I would like to sit down with him, at that small table. And I would like to tell him that I really did like his family that he made, and his house that he had, and my job in his house. I would like to tell him that I am very, very sorry that he got divorced from his wife. And I would like to listen to him, if he wanted to tell me about everything that went wrong.

I could have that conversation. I could have it. But I don't know what would happen after the conversation, and after our tea was finished. Because I would have to catch the bus back here, and walk up the street in the dark, and he would be left in the small flat above the parking lot, with two dirty cups in his sink.

But you right. The cups would be clean, because I would have rinsed them out before I left. Of course I know that. Of course.

Secret

I WENT TO THE HAIRDRESSER TODAY. I walked up the street in my lunch hour, in the noonday sun. I was persuaded to get a perm. The hairdresser says a perm is the look for the seventies. It's not the sixties anymore, she says. I don't care much.

But I suddenly remembered how it was when I first came here. I knew the town from the times I had come with my father on his truck, to get farm supplies at the wholesaler, and general supplies at Kriegler's. We used to come every week. I would see the girls going to the bioscope. I'd never been to the bioscope.

When I moved here I got a room in the Venters' house. They were an old couple, he was retired from his job at the post office, and their children had moved away, to the city I suppose. I got a job at Kriegler's shop, working the cash. It paid enough for me to cover my rent and to go to the bioscope with Connie on Saturdays. I could afford to have my hair set at the hairdresser's too, and I sew, so when I wanted something fresh I would go into Mrs Hannepoort's for a few yards of fabric and make something on my mother's sewing machine, which stood in a corner of my room, under the window.

The job at Kriegler's was all right. I used to hope that one day a handsome man would come into the store and sweep me off my feet, as Connie used to say, and marry me, and maybe we'd go and live in a real city—not Jo'burg, I couldn't imagine that, but maybe a town with pretty houses and white fences, and more shops than we have here. Connie always hoped that would happen to her too, and we did a lot of planning, me and Connie. Connie's gone now, she got married—although to a farmer—and she lives not far from here. She invites me for lunch on Sundays, her husband picks me up in his truck, and I visit and bring a little something for her kids.

I, well, I'm not married yet. I don't live at the Venters any more, and I work nowadays for Mrs Hannepoort. Mrs Hannepoort always tells me how lucky she is to have me, because I have an eye for colour and style, that's what she tells me. I do alterations on the dresses, and we are busy most of the time. Connie herself comes in here from her farm and has dresses made, and some of her neighbours do too. Mrs Hannepoort makes hats as well, which the older ladies like to wear for church.

But I'll tell you the story of what happened when I worked at Kriegler's, because I think about it. I think about it far more than I'd like. I'm not really sure why, because it had nothing to do with me. It wasn't even about old Mr Kriegler, who retired soon after then anyway.

It began one hot afternoon. I was alone at the cash, at the front of the shop. It was a dark and dusty shop, Mr Kriegler really should've cleaned it up. There were no customers and I was reading my magazine. That's how it was in the afternoons. Lunch hour was busier, then the natives came in, bought some stuff that they needed: soap, tobacco, some blankets we had.

I looked up to see a man standing in the light of the doorway. He was thin; I could see his silhouette. He walked into the shop.

He was one of the natives, except I noticed right away he had city clothes on. He wore long pants and a shirt: worn, shabby, but from the city. He was carrying a bundle. D'you have a job ma'am, he said. And the thing was, that morning Mr Kriegler had said to me, Anneline I need a boy in packing, if someone's looking for a job. So I told him to come back at five o'clock to see Mr Kriegler. And out he went into the hot sun. I could see his silhouette again, thin, dark against the bright light of the doorway.

I carried on reading my magazine. It was so hot, even inside the shop. I had to get the fly swatter also because I don't know what it is, the flies always come in the afternoon heat.

At five o'clock he came back. He was punctual. Mr Kriegler was busy at the back, and I was busier now too. My magazine was folded in my bag. I was ringing up the cash. Mrs Botha was in getting some soap and her other weeklies and she was going on about the church and the new *dominee* that we had. I was nodding and agreeing, to be polite. She goes on and on. I wasn't listening at all, and I told the boy—he said his name was Philemon—wait, I'll call Mr Kriegler.

He waited at the door. I had to call Mr Kriegler three times. He doesn't care if he keeps people waiting. Certainly not a native, in any case. I think Philemon eventually went outside, because I saw that dark silhouette again in the bright, square doorway. And there's something funny: every once in a while I dream, even these days, of that silhouette. I don't dream much. I dream of my mother, of her kneading bread in the kitchen on the farm. There was the thumping sound of the dough on the counter, as she kneaded, then lifted and pounded again. I dream of the thorn tree in the drought, that was the only tree for miles and miles, on our farm. I have another dream now, too, but I'm getting to that.

Mr Kriegler came to the front of the store at last. He took one look at Philemon. He makes fast decisions, that's how Mr Kriegler is. Let's see your pass, boy, he said. He said it in Afrikaans, which is what we speak in this town, and I could see right away that

Afrikaans was not the boy's language. I mean, I think English was his language. Not his own language, of course not. But he answered quick, I saw again, in Afrikaans. *Ja, alles goed met die paas.* Even Mr Kriegler could see then he was an English one, because Mr Kriegler switched to English after that.

So Mr Kriegler took Philemon into packing and that was that. We had three boys in packing. They had to unload the trucks at the back when they came with supplies and stock the shelves. I used to see them sitting on crates outside at lunchtime. I saw Philemon was with them, after that first day. He was quieter than the others, because he was new I suppose, but maybe because he spoke a different language, I don't know. A couple of times I saw him smoking a cigarette, standing in the yard at the back, in the shade of the roof.

He did his work, that's all I cared about. He carried the crates, he packed properly, he wasn't cheeky either. You know. After a few weeks Mr Kriegler told me he was putting Philemon in charge of the other two packers, and Philemon had to fill in the forms now, checking off the deliveries. Mr Kriegler could see he was clever, I suppose. So at the end of each day Philemon had to come and give me the forms that he'd filled in, and I had to file them away in the drawer under my counter.

One day I said to Philemon, d'you come from Jo'burg or what. I think he didn't like that question—maybe he was shy—because he frowned and shook his head. No ma'am, Vereeniging, he said, and he carried on filling in the form, checking off the list with his pen. But I liked him, he did his job, he kept to himself, so I said in a joke, hey you look like you come from Jo'burg, and you speak proper English—I heard you. That's what I said to him. No ma'am, Vereeniging, just Vereeniging I told you. He put the form on my counter and went to the back again. And then I wondered why he would come here from Vereeniging, which is a bigger town than ours. We only get people from the farms here. We're off the main

Free State road, but nobody comes here for work unless they're born here, or they come from a farm, like I do.

I would see the boys from the shop walking home from work, as I walked home to the Venters. Bye ma'am, bye ma'am they'd say. They had a long walk to the Location. I had seen the road they had to take. Just a long, straight road in the hot sun. I was sure it would take an hour, that's what I thought. I saw the corrugated iron roofs of the Location once when I went with Mr Kriegler in his truck. The roofs caught the rays of the sun. I had to shade my eyes.

And then the Friday business started. Every Friday afternoon I went to the hairdresser and had my hair done. I used to follow the fashions in my magazine. Mr Kriegler would joke with me about looking beautiful and finding a husband, and he told me to go to the hairdresser, he'd cover for me at the cash. He didn't mind, he said. He said it was good for business in any case for him to see what went on at the front. I'd see him settling himself at the till as I left.

One Friday Mr Kriegler told me Philemon was going to work at the cash and fill in for me while I was gone. Mr Kriegler was going to show him the till, and then Philemon would do it. I didn't think that was a good idea at all. What would someone like Mrs Botha say if she came in for her shopping and there was a native working at the cash? I told Mr Kriegler this. Ah, he said, that's ridiculous, I'm not worried about Mrs Botha. But usually he was very worried about Mrs Botha, very polite to her, Mrs Botha this, Mrs Botha that, telling me about good service to the customers and all that. It's only an hour you're gone, he said, and Philemon can do the job. He's good with numbers. That's what Mr Kriegler said. If you ask me, Mr Kriegler just thought it was easier for him if he didn't have to sit at the cash, and Philemon would sit there and maybe Mrs Botha wouldn't even come in then and notice. That's what I think was in Mr Kriegler's mind. Because mostly Mr Kriegler just wanted everything running smoothly in his shop, that's how he was.

But it's true about Philemon being good with numbers, because when I came back from the hairdresser I checked the cash and the receipts and all, and everything was perfect, just as if I had done it. A few weeks of that and I stopped checking altogether—I would just read my magazine when I came back.

Once I came back and saw Philemon had left a newspaper folded on the counter. I like my counter clean and clear, he was supposed to leave nothing there. And which newspaper was he reading, do you think? Because when I unfolded it I saw it was the English newspaper. And I've hardly ever seen that English newspaper in our town. I've seen some English people carrying it around, and I suppose Mr Kriegler reads it in his house where he lives with his wife, because he speaks English, but that's all.

Another time I saw Philemon reading that paper in the yard at the back. I said to him, trying to joke with him again, what's going on in Jo'burg Philemon? What's news in Jo'burg? He didn't like that question because he said, oh nothing, the usual. Then he folded up the newspaper and walked away.

Was Philemon married? How should I know? He walked home to the Location at six o'clock, and that's all I know about that. Next morning at eight o'clock sharp he was there at the shop with the other boys.

But I'll tell you what happened. One afternoon it was. It was the same kind of afternoon as when Philemon first arrived. Hot. I was fanning myself with my magazine. I was drinking from a bottle of Coke, that's how hot it was. Because usually I don't drink Coke. I said to Mr Kriegler can I buy a Coke at the front from the fridge. Just take it, he said, write a note in the till. The bottle had beads of cold water on it.

The boys at the back were quiet, they were probably sitting on the crates having a break. Mr Kriegler was in his office. He was usually on the phone in the afternoons, talking to his suppliers.

He waved me away once, when I went to him with a question. He had to get his orders in.

I was up on my stool. Suddenly the bright square of the doorway was filled. It was a policeman: his large shape and police cap were silhouetted against the light. He walked in slowly and looked around. He saw me and nodded. *Goeie middag, mevrou.* Good afternoon, madam. *Middag meneer*, I said. Afternoon, sir. He looked around again and shifted his feet. Where're your packing boys? That's what he said. Packing boys. The packing boys? I was thinking this had never happened before. I've seen the policemen on the streets—many times—stopping the boys, for their passes I suppose. But why must he come in here to check their passes? That's what I was thinking.

He said, very polite, madam please come with me out of the shop. He came around the counter and put his hand under my arm—still polite as anything, a real gentleman, and he started walking me out of the shop. He was tall and handsome too, in that uniform of his. I just walked. But then I said, *meneer*, Mr Kriegler— the boss—he's back there in his office. Yes, ma'am, thank you ma'am, he said. He learned his manners from his mother, all right, that's what I was thinking.

Next thing I found myself outside in the bright sun, and there was a police van parked there, and six or seven policemen standing, watching us come out. And another man, not in uniform, was standing there, same as the policemen, watching us come out of the door. I was a bit embarrassed in truth because it looked like I was being arrested, though I'd done nothing.

Then all the uniformed policemen went into the shop, one after the other, and now I saw they had guns. But these weren't ordinary guns. Look, I know nothing about guns, but these were big guns— machine guns. And then I heard lots of shouting inside the shop. And less than two minutes later all the policemen came out again, guns pointing, and in the middle, with his hands in the air, and saying nothing, was Philemon.

Mr Kriegler came running out. What's the problem, man, what's the problem. I've never seen him so angry. Look here, man, you can't just come into private property and take someone. Where's your boss, man? And the policemen ignored Mr Kriegler as though he was just a nuisance fly or something, and then the one who was not in uniform said to Mr Kriegler, here's my card, boss-man, give me a call if you want to talk about it. Mr Kriegler said again, come on, man, come on, what's your problem. Mr Kriegler and his grey hair looked so small next to the policemen in their uniforms, but he looked as if he wanted to hit one of them anyway.

Then I saw one of the policemen lift his baton and hit Philemon hard on his back. With all his weight and strength, because I saw it. And he hit him again. Philemon was just standing there with his hands in the air, saying nothing. Philemon—Philemon's a thin man, not even a tall man—he just fell in a heap onto the dusty ground. Mr Kriegler was red in the face and sweating and shouting at the policemen, come on, man, come on, what's the matter with you. I was sweating too, I could feel my slip stuck to the back of my legs, and the sun was shining hot in my eyes, and Philemon was in a heap in the dust.

By this time a crowd had gathered across the road. The butcher, the fat Mr Viljoen, was standing outside his shop with his white apron on, and some other natives were just standing there, looking and looking.

The policeman who had hit Philemon said *opstaan jou moer*, and I was thinking now he's swearing something terrible, and he's forgotten his manners after all, because you're not supposed to swear like that in front of a lady, and then all the policemen in their shiny shoes started moving in the dust towards the van. The policeman pulled Philemon up and pushed him into the back of the van, as if he was throwing a bag of potatoes in there, in the dark van. The man without a uniform said to Mr Kriegler, who looked now something terrible, his grey hair standing up mostly, *middag meneer*. Afternoon, sir. Then he turned to me. *Mevrou*, he said. Madam. He inclined his head. Then he got into the van and it roared off, blowing dust up behind it, into my eyes.

We all stood there. Mr Viljoen, the butcher, turned around, shaking his head, and went back into his shop. He was probably just annoyed by all the racket. The natives stood, talking in low voices. Mr Kriegler turned around and walked very fast into the shop. I was worried about him, I thought he could have a heart attack. I'd never seen him so angry. Red in the face. When I came in he was locking up the till. I'm closing early, he said. Anneline, you can go home. The óther boys at the back, he released them for the afternoon too. I saw them picking up their things, their bundles, at the back door, shaking their heads, talking quietly among themselves. Mr Kriegler said go, go Anneline, I'll see you tomorrow morning. He said he would lock up.

I went home. Mr Venter was smoking his pipe on the stoep, and he waved, but I didn't feel like talking. I went straight to my room, which was like an oven from being closed up all day.

We never saw Philemon again. Mr Kriegler told me later it was the Special Branch from Jo'burg that came and took him. They had information about him, and Philemon wasn't even his real name, Mr Kriegler said. He said Philemon was a political, and now he was probably a political prisoner, maybe even one of the famous ones, because there are famous ones, that's what Mr Kriegler told me. Famous where, I said to Mr Kriegler, but he just shook his head.

I don't know about famous prisoners, I don't know about prison and prisoners at all, because I follow the law. I asked Mr Kriegler what exactly is a political, is it a Communist. He shook his head. Ah, Anneline, Anneline, he said. Never mind. Never mind. That's what he said. But I figured it out for myself. I could see Philemon came from Jo'burg. I know about those natives—they get some education, they want to make plans to change things. I hear people talking about that, more and more now, because they're worried.

The Special Branch told Mr Kriegler be careful who you employ here, boss-man. We're watching you. That's what they told him. And perhaps they're watching me too.

Mr Kriegler retired and sold his business soon after that. It had been planned for a while because he was over seventy years old, he had grandchildren and all. I think he went to retire and sit on his stoep with his pipe, with Mrs Kriegler, just like Mr and Mrs Venter, that's what I think. The new owner kept me on at the cash because Mr Kriegler gave me a good reference, and I was there for a while longer before I started at Mrs Hannepoort's. But I still have that dream of the bright square doorway, with a dark silhouette, of him, of the one who came to work at Kriegler's that day.

There's something else. I've thought a lot about it. I see now there are things that nobody told me. Not my mother, and not my father. Not my schoolteachers in the district school, and not the *dominee* in our church; not my magazine which comes out every week, and not even the films I see on Saturdays, that are made in America, far away. Even the newspaper—our newspaper—that I look at once in a while, never told me this. If the Special Branch has to arrest politicals, that's one thing. But Philemon was standing in the hot sun with his arms up in the air. Why, oh why, did the policeman in his uniform, and his shoes so shiny, hit Philemon with all his strength? And why—because I remember it now—why did he kick him, as he lay in a heap in the dust? And—I remember this too—the thud of Philemon's body when they threw him in the van. And this I dream about at night—what happened after that? Because there's a place—I do know about it, after all. It's the headquarters of the Special Branch, and it's in Jo'burg, and it's a famous place, it's in a big building, and they do whatever the hell they like in that building. It's a secret, but it's not a secret. How can that be?

It's a secret. A large—a massive—secret. It's everywhere. How can that be?

It's a secret I saw once. As the sun struck my eyes, like a blow.

Our Story / His Story

S OMETIME IN THE SUMMER OF 1975 we had a visitor. Not an ordinary visitor. We had many ordinary visitors. There was our grandmother who came for tea—bearing sweets—on Sunday afternoons. There were our friends who came to play and swim in the pool. There were mom and dad's guests, a perfumed procession on Saturday nights, who laughed and tinkled glasses into the still air of the patio, the patio that glinted whitely under the faraway stars. No. Sometime in the summer of 1975 a different visitor came.

It all started with Elias. Elias cleaned the pool and took care of the garden. He lived in a room at the back. He washed the cars on Fridays, hauling the hose to the front, with the buckets and rags. One day Elias asked dad if Jimmy could come and stay for a few weeks in his room at the back. Jimmy? Dad had never heard of Jimmy before. Jimmy. My son. From the farm. Mom had heard from time to time about Jimmy. Dad said of course Jimmy could come and stay. He would go back to his mother after, Elias said. His mother? Yes, his mother. Of course. Of course.

Dad thought afterwards that Jimmy could not be his real name. Jimmy was my brother's (that's Jonathan's) nickname—we've called him that since infancy. Elias's Jimmy must have a Xhosa name, was what dad was thinking later when he was in his clinic attending to a patient. And after he thought about it, he could see how Elias would want his son to grow up like our Jimmy. Strong and handsome. Healthy. Clever. Dad could see that.

And so it was arranged. Jimmy would come and visit. Elias took three days off work to get him. It was far, where Jimmy lived. There was a train, we had heard discussion about that.

And so it was that one ordinary day in the summer of 1975, we trooped home from school to find a small black boy seated at the kitchen table. We put down our bags. Evelyn, who worked in the kitchen, had given Jimmy a mug of tea and some bread and apricot jam. The bread, a thick white slice, was untouched. Jimmy's wide eyes stared at us over the rim of his mug. We stared too.

Dad came home from work later with his doctor's bag, and the newspaper folded under his arm. Usually he went to change before he poured himself a drink and sat down with his crossword. But that day he came straight into the kitchen to see Jimmy. He took Jimmy on his knee. Hi, Jimmy. Hi. Jimmy said not a word. He didn't speak English. That's what Evelyn said. Does he eat Elias, dad said. Does he eat? Elias spread his arms in a gesture of helplessness. Evelyn pursed her lips and said nothing. We looked at Jimmy. He was small; he was six years old. But he was too small. Even we could see that. And we heard dad tell mom that night as well. He's too small for his age. Too small.

We heard the murmurings from mom and dad's room later, when we were supposed to be asleep. Usually I ignored their talk, its rise and fall in the quiet of the house. But that night, in the dark of my room, I lay awake, listening. There were murmurings about

Elias, and about Jimmy. Elias, Jimmy. There'd be a silence, and then they'd start up again. There was mention of the farm. A mystery, there. And another word, which filled the silence, the close darkness of our night-time house. Malnutrition. It was such an ugly word.

We live in a different country now. You know that, of course. Not too much has changed for us. We still have visitors (ordinary ones), and parties sometimes. Pools don't glitter so in this northern light, I've told you that too. But there are sweets and perfumes; tinkling glasses.

Last week, when we gathered for dinner, someone mentioned the visit from Jimmy that summer of 1975. We started talking about it. We seem to remember that Jimmy stayed for two weeks. That's what we remember. What we remember is that Jimmy slept in Elias's room at the back. He played in the yard, and he played with us when we came home from school. And after two weeks (as we remember it), Elias took Jimmy back to the farm to his mother. He never visited again. Those, I think, are the facts of the visit.

But we all remember facts differently. My sister remembers very little. Oh that, she says, on the subject of Jimmy (with a toss of the head). She remembers other things: things about school, about her friends. Things that belong in quite a different story than this one.

I remember that mom spent two weeks bustling around the kitchen with Evelyn, talking about protein, about milk. About feeding Jimmy. Evelyn (I see her now, in my mind's eye) removed her glasses and cleaned them on her apron. She was not at all sure what could be achieved by feeding Jimmy.

Mom had a plan to feed Jimmy. I remember her shopping and telling Evelyn this and that. I remember that she told dad every night how much success she was having, feeding Jimmy. She had a pink spot high on each cheek, when she told him. Dad was quieter than usual, I remember that too.

Mom, for her part, remembers the silence between Evelyn and herself. Evelyn's silence, and the kitchen, and the subject of Jimmy's diet, gone over and over with Evelyn, who pursed her lips and shook her head. Mom didn't tell us this last week, when we were remembering, but I know this is what she remembers. She remembers going to her room with a headache. She remembers lying in the quiet of her room. She remembers the hush; the stillness of her room.

Dad gave Elias a bottle of vitamins and other supplements for Jimmy. He remembers that. I remember that, too. But perhaps, after examining Jimmy, dad did something else. Perhaps he took Jimmy to his clinic in the car one day. Perhaps I saw Jimmy's small black head at the back of the car as it drove up the street to the clinic. A secretary there kept track of people's health in many brown files; kept track of children's weight and height and vaccinations and pills. Perhaps dad opened a brown file for Jimmy and put his name on the front. Perhaps he recorded the facts about Jimmy's height and his weight, and gave Elias other things for Jimmy to take, to ensure that he would grow up healthy and strong.

And perhaps, after the visit to his clinic, dad gave money to Elias. Perhaps he increased his pay by many times: the money in a brown envelope that he gave him at the end of each month. Perhaps I saw the brown envelope filled to bulging, and to bursting. Perhaps I did not.

And perhaps dad signed Elias's much creased and faded pass book in a certain way, so that Jimmy could stay in our house at all. Because now I know that that is what dad would have had to do, to make sure that police didn't come and take Elias away, for keeping Jimmy in his room. Perhaps Elias was lucky, and the police weren't patrolling our street during those two weeks in the summer of 1975. Or perhaps, finding them, the police felt compassion for a black man and a six-year-old boy, hiding in the dark of a room. Perhaps the police drew the line at taking a boy's father in the dead of night. And perhaps they did not.

And if dad signed the pass book, and took Jimmy to his clinic, and increased Elias's pay, then perhaps he did other things too. Perhaps he thought about protesting and doing illegal things that would land him in jail. And perhaps he did not. Perhaps he lives with the knowledge that he is no hero, after all. I can guess that he voted in an election to defeat a government that made laws that kept children like Jimmy away from their fathers, and I can guess he saw how useless that was.

I like to think that dad did everything that was in his power to do. But that is merely my wish. Whether or not he did everything that was in his power to do, I will never know, because dad doesn't say. And I know, now, how limited dad's power was, in the story of Elias and Jimmy, so I have to forgive him too.

And Jonathan (whom we called, with love, Jimmy). Jonathan doesn't say what he remembers, and sometimes he claims he doesn't remember at all. But he surely remembers how Jimmy laughed when we played because I remember that. And he bears within him, I am certain, an image of Jimmy, who was his namesake after all. An image of a small, black Jimmy, not one strong and white, like himself. A strange mirror image that stands next to his own. Like a younger brother, perhaps one he never asked for, but a brother all the same. Jonathan is not one to talk about things like that. You know Jonathan, so you know that too.

And there's Evelyn. Evelyn adjusts her glasses as she remembers Jimmy's arms, and his legs that dangled from the chair where he sat in her kitchen. She remembers the slices of bread, oh she remembers them all right. You may ask how I know this, because Evelyn is not with us here, she was not remembering this with us last week, from a different place. But I know it. I see Evelyn adjusting her glasses. I see her inward sigh. Even now.

And Elias. Elias with his upturned, spread-out arms, who had no answer at all. What can one say of Elias, who brought Jimmy, after all?

Then there's Jimmy himself. I have told you, just now, the story of what we remember, when we had our visitor in the summer of 1975. I have tried, anyway. But Jimmy's story is the one I want to tell you most of all. It's the story that interests me the most.

I would tell you about the farm Jimmy came from: dust; some chickens; a corrugated iron roof shimmering in the afternoon heat. That is all. Or that is all I can tell you, because I never went there. So you can see that Jimmy's story is the one that I myself cannot tell. And there's something else: I think it's Jimmy's story to tell. I am far away now, but I am certain Jimmy will tell his story one day. Perhaps, if you listen, you will hear it.

What She Carried

HE RECEPTIONISTS WORKED SHIFTS: seven to three, and three to eleven. There was she—Janine—and there was Estelle. They alternated. Estelle wore lots of make-up and was pretty, auburn-haired. She was vivacious too, with a touch of glamour. The guests loved her. "Good morning, sir," she would say with her smile that was a laugh. She would engage in small talk: the weather, the guests' health. Janine, on the other hand, was not as good at small talk, and not as vivacious. She was moody. The mornings got to her: getting up at six, hitching a ride to the hotel to arrive by seven. Hitch-hiking. Not such a good idea. Not at the best of times, and not at six-thirty on Sea Point Road on a chill Cape Town morning. She had a plan always. Hand on the door handle, ready to yank the door open if necessary. It never had been necessary, up until that point. But still.

Janine liked the other hotel staff, usually. There was Mrs Nel, the housekeeper, who had seen better days—working in other, better hotels, she had told Janine, many times. And there was

John, gap-toothed and insolent, who would stand leaning his elbows on the reception desk, which is not how he was supposed to stand, as a hotel porter, at all. There was Anju, the house manager. He had an aquiline face, and deep brown eyes. Janine relied on Anju. Problem with a reservation? Anju would fix it in no time. Problem with an irate customer? Anju would know what to do.

The hotel itself had seen better days. Once it had been a hub for holiday-makers on the fashionable beach front. Now, with its faded crimson drapes and carpet, she was a dowager in need of repair. Now the customers were mostly corporate (as they called them). They were software engineers (said Mrs Nel), businessmen attending conferences or meetings. Airlines put their staff up there too. Estelle liked the airline customers. They were glamorous, she said.

Janine noticed the sous-chef soon after he started working there. She'd see him in his blue-and-white striped chef's jacket coming in, and leaving at the end of his shift. His straight black hair was in need of a trim, she thought, his black-rimmed glasses often steamed up. He intrigued her. She saw him one day leaving in an old, beaten-up car. She heard the engine stuttering as he drove away. It was John, the porter, whistling through his teeth, who said it was the car's muffler gone. Janine knew nothing about cars.

She saw him sometimes leaving work with the other sous-chef—the German. They were a pair, in their chef's jackets: one dark-haired, and one blonde. Estelle had no interest in them. Estelle was interested in the pilots from the airlines, in fancy cars (she said), and in the software engineers. Janine kept her eye on the sous-chef, and didn't say a word about him to Estelle.

One day he noticed her. Maybe he needed something from reception, for the kitchen. Maybe he needed to ask something. Janine doesn't remember. But suddenly he was at her desk, speaking to her. After that he came almost every day to the reception desk, on his way to or from his shift. She knew he was coming especially to speak with her. And John, grinning, would be watching, making wisecracks—as Mrs Nel called them.

One day the sous-chef asked if she wanted to go for a drink after work. With him and his friend, the other sous-chef. She went with them to a bar across the road. It was in a restaurant, filled with people on holiday. Not working people like them, from the hotel. It was busy; jostling. Janine had a Coke. She watched him, his dark eyes flashing behind his glasses, with their heavy rims. He laughed. They talked about work, about the hotel. He drove her home afterwards, in the car with the muffler gone, and then drove away with his friend.

And that became regular, a drink after work (but no drink for her). And then always he drove her home, in his beaten-up old car. Once the car didn't start at all, and they had to wait for another friend of his to come and pick them up. And there was a long discussion, under the hood of the car, about the exhaust, about the garage, while Janine stood and waited on the curb.

Mrs Nel had her views about men with broken cars. Views about the prospects of men with broken cars. She did not hesitate to air them to Janine. Janine cared not at all. Janine had left her own mother's house for one reason, at least, and that was that she didn't want someone else's views about things. About men; about prospects. About anything at all.

What interested her was, what it was like in the kitchen, where he worked. Once she stood for a moment at the wide double door. Steam billowed out toward her. There was the gleam of the steel counters and ovens. There was the sizzle and sputter of the grill, and its smoke, and the dull hum of the refrigerator, whose heavy door opened and closed with a thunk and a thud. There was the roar of the gas extractor. And there was the noise of men shouting: orders, instructions, curses, jokes. And the cooks, the juniors, yelling, tossing things around, laughing together. It was a cauldron of a place. She saw him there, at the grill. His glasses streaked; a sheen of sweat on his face.

And, even when he was finished work, and he was driving the car, his eyes on the road as she sat beside him (mesmerized), he smelled of the kitchen. An aura of cooking; of the grill. It bothered her not at all. He was lean and strong, and she fell in love with him. He spoke in a soft, hesitant voice, and he swore a lot. That was fine with her too (even though she—she—didn't swear much at all).

He lived in a rented room with a side entrance in a house; she in a flat along Sea Point Road. Maybe sous-chefs earned more money than receptionists, but he sank quite a bit of money into his beaten-up old car, and now, she saw, he had some other bad habits too. He smoked a lot. Not at work. But at home, all the time. She never smoked.

In his room, bare of all adornment (a pock-marked wall, a bed, just a bed), where they went after their shift, he told her that he'd got into trouble once, and owed someone money. What d'you mean, she said. Oh, I've got to pay him every month, he said, don't worry about it. She didn't worry about it. It was one of the things he told her that was a piece of something else. She discarded it. They made love until dawn.

Once he surprised her by going away for a few days, by plane. He said he had to take care of something in Johannesburg to do with his brother. She didn't know he had a brother. It's too complicated to explain, he said. She knew about some things being too complicated to explain, and, later, she discarded that too.

One night, at eleven when both their shifts ended, he said he was going to visit his friends in Langa. Did she want to come? Come with me, he said. Janine knew Langa only by name. Most people only knew Langa by name, from the newspapers. Langa: where the coloureds lived, on the barren flats that stretched north of Cape Town. It was dangerous—filled with crime—in Langa.

That's what she knew. She had an image of her mother's pale face, and its small frown. She erased it, with a stroke. Yes, she would go with him to Langa.

They drove from the lights of the city and were soon on the highway, north. They turned, later, onto a dirt road, and followed it, slower now. It went straight, bumping into nowhere. It veered, sharply, once; then again. The car spattered stones. She wasn't sure how he could see the road, because there were no lights now, and there was nothing to be seen, no road or path, no house or person. There was just the black sky arching overhead, and the two of them in the car. The car's engine sputtered. And finally: a destination, which looked to her just a clearing. Not in the trees, because there were no trees. Just a clearing set away from the road, next to nothing.

She looked at him. There was his profile, darkly etched. And after she had got out of the car and stood with him, she saw that they were somewhere, after all. There was a wood fire, and around it a ring of chairs, or an assortment of upturned barrels and boxes. And men, dark shadows, moving faintly against the orange of the fire, like marionettes. There was a radio playing music, with a dim beat. Cigarettes glowed, like animals' eyes. There was the heavy, sweet smell of marijuana. And a haze of smoke over it all.

She wondered about what she had done, agreeing to come here. She thought about how far she was, now, from the lights, the familiarity of the city. She thought of the dark highway behind them.

She remembers herself—when she thinks about it now—as a silent presence at his side. Featureless, in the dark. But female. And protected by him. He greeted everyone, spoke and laughed. The men, the shadows, addressed him by name. They shook hands, in that strange double-handed shake she'd seen before. He had said they were his friends. They looked like his friends.

The men ignored her, although she knew some were talking about her, in their broken mixed-up language. But respectfully talking; they were respectful. This, she knew, was because she was with him. Or, rather, she sensed this, because she didn't know much at all.

They sat around the fire. A breeze lifted her hair. The talk around her rose and fell. Sometimes she could understand it, and sometimes she couldn't. She felt the warmth of his body next to hers. Hand against hand, arm against arm. She could feel his voice vibrate softly, next to her. She was lulled. She watched the fire.

And then, he stood up abruptly, to go. There was more hand-shaking. Farewells. She heard her voice saying, g'bye, goodbye. She remembers stumbling in a rut next to the car, the sound of her car door slamming shut, and her hand pushing down the lock button, fast. And he started the car with a sputter, and they set off home.

They were silent in the car. There was the dark, rutted road again, and the car bumping along it. And finally the highway. They sped then. The lights of the city rose to greet them. A deliverance. And she told him she wasn't going there again, if he didn't mind. And that was fine with him too.

When she thought about it afterwards, and she did think about it afterwards, Janine had an idea he went to Langa at other times too. With the other sous-chef—the German—sometimes, and sometimes alone. Why he did this, she didn't know. They were his friends in Langa. That's what he told her.

And after he was gone, she thought about that. About what he had told her, and about what he hadn't. During her shift in the faded, crimson lobby of the hotel, she thought about it. She remembered the shadowy men around the fire. And she saw it now: how they waited for him, and the expectancy she felt coming from them, like a scent. They were waiting for him because they were waiting for something from him. Of course. Waiting and waiting for him. And how they turned themselves to him, like flowers, when he came. He had power over them. He sold them drugs. That's what he did. He was their supplier, their contact. Their man. He sold them drugs. And all of that, he hadn't told her.

He's in prison now, and how strange it sounds when she says that. There was a short trial, where she went, in support. She sat on a wooden bench, and as the sun came through the high window of the courtroom she watched the back of his head in the dock in front of her. She twisted and untwisted the purse straps on her lap, she remembers that.

So he's gone, and he won't be back. This was going to happen eventually, that's what Jan (the German, the other sous-chef) says. He's her friend now, they speak after their shift sometimes. Jan knew what was going on in Langa; he knew all about it. She asks him why he didn't tell her, and he shrugs. Mrs Nel shakes her head. She had a bad feeling about him from the beginning, she says. A bad feeling. That car of his. That's what she keeps saying, as she stands with her clipboard at the desk, checking off rooms. And Estelle. Estelle purses her glossy lips when the subject of the drug-dealer sous-chef (as she calls him) comes up. And her eyes, already, are on the pilots striding in their uniforms across the lobby. Like a magpie's, after gold.

But Janine goes over and over in her mind the things that he had told her and the things that he hadn't. As if it were a puzzle, with a missing piece. Something she missed. And she had missed what was essential, it seemed. How could she? And yet. Was the essential not his smile, or his laughing eyes behind his glasses that flashed? How she puzzles over it, now this way, now that, as if turning it a different way, in a different light, will show a different answer: a new, clean, face.

And doing this, one time (going over and over in her mind the things he had said, and the things he hadn't), she remembers—suddenly—something very important. How could she have forgotten it? There was a package, once. She remembers, now, the package he gave her to carry home, along Sea Point Road, those months ago. He didn't tell her what was in it, and she didn't ask.

He had said, as they were leaving work, can you take this home for me, and I'll pick it up later. I have to go somewhere now, take it for me. She remembers the casualness of his voice, its softness and gentleness. It held her in a spell. Of course she'd take it.

She remembers the hot, damp air along Sea Point Road; her warm damp face, and the strands of hair that clung limply to her forehead. She remembers the sound of the sea advancing and receding beyond the sea wall. There was her breathing, which advanced and receded too. She remembers the weight of the package, which she held with both hands. It was a small weight, an insignificant weight, yet she held it with both hands (or perhaps that is merely how she remembers it). How important she felt, entrusted with the package. A carrier. A bearer. Loved and trusted; carrier, bearer.

And he did come to her flat later, long past midnight, to pick the package up and take it away. Thanks, he had said. He had whispered it, because it was late, and she was half asleep. And he had kissed her, lightly, leaning over her. The stubble grazed her cheek. And it comes to her what was in the package. The cargo of drugs she carried. And she sees herself, a small figure breathing hot sea air under the lights along Sea Point Road. A small figure who was not stopped by police on her route that night, but a small figure (damp face, damp hair) who might have been stopped all the same.

And later, much later, she would carry something for someone else. Nine months that time. Loved and entrusted; carrier, bearer. And she would be reminded again of the package he gave her on Sea Point Road, all that time ago. The package she carried. It signaled some kind of love, didn't it? She's not at all sure.

Wan

THE GRAPEFRUIT WAS SHARP in my mouth when I read the report. I was on the terrace, the morning sun filtering through the trees—a hot, still day it would be. It was the kind of news we read all the time, back then. Attempted sabotage of power plant. Et cetera. I got tired of it. I turned to the theatre listings—I was to book tickets for a play.

And then I went in to dress. There was my face, wan in the morning light, I remember it, that day.

My husband mentioned it a few days later. He said there was a colleague's friend who needed somewhere to stay—a few weeks, that was all. Someone involved in the recent attempt. He'd stay in the garden room, there was a bathroom there, we'd not need to see him. I was irritated. Is this necessary Howard, I said. It's necessary, yes, he said, you know it's necessary. We had had someone else like that stay once in that room. My husband was not afraid; I was not either. He thought the police would never touch him. I told the servants a man from Howard's work would be in the room for a few weeks. They weren't much interested, of course. I told them not to bother him, he'd take care of the room himself.

A few days later he came home with my husband. He shook my hand. Thank you, thank you, he said. I'll be moving on soon. It'll be all right, my husband said, it'll be fine. The three of us had a drink. It was a strange time, then.

And then I forgot about it. Or I tried to forget about it. I did not see him. Howard said he had books with him. He was a university professor, before. At night, very late, he had visitors, the servants told me that. The visitors came in cars, headlights pooling in the darkness, they let themselves in at the side gate. I never heard them. My husband assured me, again, he'd be gone soon.

I had my own preoccupations. The children, both, finally away at university. I was free. I was working, then, on my series—the white series. You've seen it. It was before then that I started it.

I wanted to create a painting that was a space, just a space. I had an image in my mind of a large white canvas, and no line, no mark to deface it or cross it. The canvas would contain its own light. Not a bright light, but a white light. D'you see what I mean? And the shape, the rectangular shape, the straight lines, the right angles of their intersections at the corners. I had been struggling, struggling so long to create this painting. I had made so many canvasses, each one defaced, despoiled in some way—a line that strayed in, the wrong shade of white, of cream, of ivory, wrong, wrong. How anguished I was. I struggled with it every morning. The light poured in through the large window—it was that light, yes, that I wanted to capture on the canvas.

At lunch time I'd emerge from the room, hands spattered with paint, as with blood. I'd have my avocado, sliced. The lemon glistened. Then I'd drink my coffee. The servants glided, here and there. They did their work. I think they did their work. The house, in any event, was in order.

I'd go out, then, in my car. The air inside was close and warm. The car was a space, an empty space, and an engine, alive. I did an errand or two. Sometimes I went to the hairdresser. I'd watch my face in the mirror, and my hair that fell, a smooth wave, on my shoulder.

In the late afternoons I would be in my bedroom, where I lay down in the silence. It was then that the image of the canvas would come to me. I would say the image haunted me, like a shadow, but it was a light shadow, and I've never seen one of those. Its largeness, and squareness. A rectangle, actually, was my canvas. I would think about which shades to try, tomorrow. Which faint gradation to choose; it mattered so much.

I was not supposed to be aware of him, staying in the garden room. I never saw him at all. But I felt his presence, down there at the end of the garden. The room was a white-washed brick, shaded by deep trees, you could see only bits of it if you looked. I wondered what he was doing there in the room all day, behind the trees, in the shadows of the trees that bent. He was working, of course, it was work he was doing: planning, writing. I thought I could hear his pen scratching on paper through the long afternoon. But I didn't hear him, of course. Then I came to see his face, stubbled, and his dark eyes, in my mind.

He was a slight man; I started to worry about what he had to eat in the room. His visitors—comrades, I should say—brought him food at night, and there was a small fridge in his room. I imagined bread and cheese. Water, water, of course. And there was his bed. I knew that bed, my son's narrow old bed with the springs that creaked. He would be able to hear the soft sigh of the trees from where he was, and his room would be dim—emerald-dim—in the afternoons, from the shade of the trees outside.

I pictured myself walking across the shadowed expanse of lawn to the room. I pictured the worn wooden door.

* * *

I told Howard he had to go, I couldn't stand it. Howard didn't understand. You never see him, you never hear him, he said. What's the problem, what's the problem. The problem was, his presence oppressed me, I came to feel it as a weight, a weight. I was used to the room being empty, somehow the garden room being empty satisfied me, I can't say why. Now there was the scratch of his pen, I heard it. For God's sake, Howard said. No one's asking you to be involved, even I'm not involved. He's going soon, forget about it, forget about it.

I tried, I did try to forget about it.

Every morning, as before, I made my way into my painting room, to my canvas. But now I balked when I saw it. It loomed at me, no light within it, I saw that now. I struggled with it, trying different things, different things. But the colour eluded me, the colour I sought.

At night I lay next to Howard. He in the garden room, on the narrow bed, shifting. I listened for the visitors, the comrades, but I never heard them. Howard slept on. I hated him, then.

And there were the newspapers. Morning after morning they were there, with their reports. Reports about the saboteurs, who were thought to be overseas. I'd sit on the terrace with my coffee. The trees stirred.

I thought, then, I would not read the newspapers any more. That was an idea, I would try that, yes.

But the newspapers, the headlines, remained.

The servants moved, hither and thither, slowly. More slowly. The garden room was filled with the sound of a scratching pen, it was filled with many things.

I abandoned my canvas. I couldn't go near it. Instead I spent many hours in my room. Sometimes, during the day, I would sleep. Then I would wake with a start. I heard scratching, the scratching of a pen. One of the servants brought me tea. Howard told me there was a delay with moving the man, to another safe place. The afternoons wore on.

And then it came to me, on one of those afternoons, what I would do. The idea was quite startling, but so clear I could hardly believe I'd not thought of it before.

I nursed the idea for many days, like a vision. I would do it.

The morning—the morning I chose—came. I got up at dawn. I combed my hair at the mirror, my hair so beautiful. It lay like a snake on my shoulder, and it's true, that morning it frightened me, just a little. The curve, and the weight of it, glossy on my shoulder. I had beautiful hair, then.

I gave the servants dinner instructions, as always. Then I got into my car and drove. Rather slowly, I drove. I didn't drive to the hairdresser down the street, or to the greengrocer, or to the paint store, with its shelves of tubes and bottles, a little further away. But I didn't drive aimlessly through the streets, as I sometimes did, just so. I drove into town. It took a little time, not much time. There was no traffic, after all. Ten o'clock in the morning, everyone at work, or at school. The buildings loomed, corner after corner, traffic light after traffic light. I drove straight to the building that I knew to be the police headquarters. I knew where it was, everyone knew where it was. I parked. I walked to the building. There was a sense of ceremony to my entry. The doorway was a double one, and high. I walked through it and up to the counter. I rested my arms—my bare arms—on it. The young man in uniform looked up. Madam, he said. Perhaps he had never seen someone like me in there before. I am certain he had never seen someone like me there before. I have to report something, I said.

They took me into an inner office, then, and sat me down. They offered me tea. Men, of course, all men. No, thank you, I said. And then I told them where to find him. I told them my husband knew nothing about it, it was me, just me, who'd let him stay there, unwittingly. But now I knew, I said, I knew who he was. I described the garden room, its bed, its fridge, its window, the trees. I described the garden room, again: its stone floor. I heard my own voice as I spoke. I have a very soft voice, I think.

They came for him in the garden room in the dead of night. We slept through it. The servants told us about it in the morning, they were very rattled. That's how they always do it, in the dead of night, Howard told me. He doesn't know how they found him, it's something I've never told him, not ever since. And we are old, now.

But my canvas. You've seen it, you know it, it's in the gallery. I completed it, yes. It's a large white rectangle. It's perfect, as I envisioned it. It is unviolated by any line or smudge or mark. Unviolated. Inviolate. Inviolable. I made the painting, I did it, I did it, and you can see it, you can see it, you can see it. What else could I do, I ask you, I ask you. I have no answer, and I am old now, old.

Counting the Days

HER GRANDMOTHER PLAYED LAWN BOWLS every afternoon. The girl watched from the window as she drove away in her car. The car jerked a little, because her grandmother was angry. The girl imagined her feet on the foot pedals of the car. The brown bowls shoes, laced-up, the stockings above them. The white skirt with pleats, and the wrinkled sun-brown hands on the wheel. The girl imagined her grandmother's head, under its curls that were set at the hairdresser's, as being a little disordered, because she was irritated with her granddaughter.

The problem started with the phone calls. She met Churchill Seroke one day on a student exchange. He was selected to visit her school in the leafy suburbs of Johannesburg. There was a speech about building bridges; about reconciliation. There was polite applause.

Churchill's skin was very black, and his behaviour very proper. He spoke English carefully. He was learning Shakespeare in school; he liked Shakespeare. She liked Shakespeare too.

After the day of the exchange, when she gave him her phone number, she wondered how this would work. She was staying, temporarily, in her grandmother's flat, her parents and sister already in London. Soon she would leave the country too. In sixty-one days. She'd been counting, marking off each day on the calendar.

Churchill called her grandmother's flat. His voice—its accented English, a black man's voice—was unmistakable to her grandmother. I won't have it, she said. Tell him not to call. But Churchill continued to call. They had long conversations, she cross-legged on the bed in her room. They spoke mostly about school, about Shakespeare. She didn't tell him she was halfway to London, her future mapped out. Drama school, maybe Oxford: an English life.

The laws forbade meeting in a public place. No movies, no restaurants. Laws forbade meeting in private places too. So they spoke on the phone, she in her grandmother's flat, he in Soweto. But where exactly? Where would he call from? He didn't have a phone. He must have been calling from a pay phone. That's as she imagined it.

Her grandmother muttered to herself. This is not at all in order. It's quite out of order, she said. It was possibly even against the law to be talking on the phone with a black man. That's what she meant to say, the girl thought, but she didn't say that.

The flat was hushed and still. There were china cups in the glossy wooden display, and figurines of glass. Silver candlesticks glinted softly in the filtered light, as it came through the netting at the window. The netting billowed in the breeze when the window was open.

On Thursdays there was no lawn bowls. Her grandmother had three ladies visit to play bridge. Tea was set out on the dining room table with the china cups. The girl stayed in her room. She'd hear the doorbell ringing and the ladies' greetings in soft voices, like birds. Soon after she'd hear the squeaking of the bridge chairs, soft laughter, and then silence. They settled into their bridge game. The girl took out her homework.

Often she didn't concentrate. With the netting billowing at the window, she would lie on her bed, doing nothing at all. She was in a limbo: neither here, nor there. She was not in England, where she was going, but she was not in South Africa either. Not really. She was in a room with a billowing white net curtain. She tried to imagine Churchill, her new friend. It would be hot where he was: a haze hanging; corrugated iron creaking and sighing. Barefoot children in the dust, and the glint of an armoured vehicle across a stretch of dun ground. Her mind alighted—rested—on the stretch of dun ground. It stayed there.

She would start again on her homework. The phone would ring. Sometimes, it was Churchill. She would know because she would hear the click of the pay phone. She imagined him putting the coin in, and she would hear his voice, slightly indistinct. They would talk. About what they were studying, and about the exams. And then: about South Africa. Sometimes the pay phone didn't work. She would hear a series of clicks, and then silence. And other times, he would be cut off in the middle, as though he'd been called away.

She imagined him in the store, where she thought the phone would be. A store with small windows, at a corner on a narrow, rutted road. A mangy dog on a chain. The afternoon hanging, while children played in the dust outside. And the phone, grimy grey, that sometimes worked and often did not. And she imagined him leaving the store afterwards, on a long, hot walk home. In her mind she followed his figure, darkly wavering in the haze, as he walked into the distance.

Every morning she went to school. She wore a uniform, pressed into pleats. Her homework was done, essays written in her careful print. She engaged with her friends: noncommittal; reserved. Sometimes when she came home there'd be a blue aerogram from her parents or her sister. It would be filled with stories, anecdotes, about life in England, where it was green and cool. Where it was green and cool, and where everything important or interesting was. That's what she thought. She was counting the days to when she'd be there.

Where she was, meanwhile, there was rising, muted, unease. Her grandmother read the newspapers, which had reports of unrest, then riots. The riots were suppressed. Her grandmother talked on the phone herself, sometimes at length, with her friends. She didn't tell them a young man (a boy) from Soweto was calling her granddaughter. This is really not in order, she said. Not in order at all. If your father knew, she said. My father would be quite pleased, the girl said. Quite pleased. He didn't really come into this at all, any more.

The girl took perverse pleasure in annoying her grandmother this way. She wanted to shake things up. Things were all wrong. They had always been wrong, over here. That's why they were leaving, after all. And it was her grandmother's generation that was responsible. At night, she lay thinking about all this: back and forth, and back and forth, round and round, and round and round again. Sometimes she was quite dizzy with it. The white netting hung, still, in the dark. No breeze came.

And her mind would reach across the city, where no breeze stirred, to where he was, and to the stretch of dun ground, in darkness now. It was a darkness, she imagined, with pinpricks of sallow light: paraffin lamps lit behind small, dim panes. She imagined him, his face a gleam in the half-light. A book open on his lap, and he reading and reading into the night. There would be a dog barking far off, and the smell of coalfires, acrid. She carried it, the acrid smell, with her the next morning to school.

She told her grandmother there was something wrong with her. Could she go to the doctor? The dizziness. Sometimes she was dizzy in the mornings too.

The doctor said she was anxious. About the exams, he said. And missing her parents, of course. And she's impatient to join them, her grandmother added. The girl said nothing.

And then Churchill would call. She felt an invisible thread, pulled. She didn't tell him she was going to England, and that became a heavy load, itself invisible, that hung on the thread that connected them. It would be a betrayal if he knew. Because she was escaping, wasn't she. Escaping, free of all this. So she dissembled. She spoke with him about Shakespeare.

To her parents in England she wrote letters about her studies, about her friends (but not about Churchill). She was a dissembler there, too. A dissembler, she saw it, everywhere.

Sometimes she had the strange sense that she had conjured him —a dark ghost—from her imagination. He didn't exist in her letters, or in her conversations at school with her friends. He wasn't supposed to exist for her, at all. It was a visitation from a different place when he called. He called; and kept calling. A calling, to her alone.

They spoke on the telephone about political change that was not coming. About forcing change. About the Movement, underground. They were conversations in low, tentative voices. Perhaps she had imagined those too.

And talking—thinking—about the Movement (which they dared not name) and its revolutionary aims, she began to worry that she would endanger her grandmother, and the other people in her neighbourhood. She saw them, elderly white ladies on their way to lawn bowls or bridge. She was colluding with the forces of revolution against them, isn't that what she was doing? That was what she was doing.

She read, in the newspaper that lay on the table at breakfast, about the kind of surveillance that security police conducted, on ordinary people just like her. She read, and read, about all of that. One afternoon she watched a white car, and a man in it, outside her window. She watched and watched. Then it drove away. She must have imagined it.

Later she became afraid of the telephone, which crouched, blackly, on a table in the hallway. When it rang—a strange, compelling power—she would start. It was calling, yes, calling. Often it was one of her grandmother's friends: a trilling, wavering, female voice. She, with trembling relief, would have a polite, short conversation and take a message.

And some days she thought that Churchill must have befriended her, not because she was a schoolgirl with ordinary interests in common with his, but because she was a pathway for him into a forbidden, white world. Perhaps he had been sent by the Movement to enlist her, or to deceive her. That possibility struck her with a new force. Perhaps he was a dissembler, a liar, too. Like her. They were liars—traitors—both.

There were reports, more often now, of riots, and of small sabotages in towns far away. An explosion in a police station on the main Reef road. She imagined parcels and packages in places unseen. She scanned the newspaper every morning, turning the pages to find a message, or a clue.

And yet: he was her friend. In another, ordinary world, he was the friend she had made. She held, she clung to that. It was an instinct as sure and strong as that to preserve her own self.

The dizziness became worse. Her grandmother took her to the doctor again. She's very anxious to be there, her grandmother said. The doctor said it wasn't long now, just take it easy, all right? He looked at her over the top of his glasses. In her head, the whirling, the dizziness, slowed. And she marked another day in pencil on the calendar.

One day, just before she was to write her exams and less than a month away from her departure (her flight already booked by her father), Churchill called. The conversation, this time, was different. I cannot call you again, he said. I'm leaving. There was the small metallic click of the phone line. Where are you going? (But she knew, already, where he was going. She knew about training camps for freedom fighters—terrorists—in Lusaka; about a headquarters for the Resistance, far away.) I'm leaving, he said again. You know. Yes. Yes. But no. No. She thought about his exams. About Shakespeare. About all the things, the many things, to be lost. A succession of things that formed a long line into the future, in her head.

She tried many times that day and after to remember what it was she had said to him in reply, because it was so important to her, to remember what she had said. And she composed, many times, things that she might have said, or should have said, or could have said. But she could not remember what she had said. The words, if she had said any, had simply flown away. And she stood in the place with the white netting, and the figurines of glass that refracted and bent the light, and the china cups that had come—she saw it now—from England, after all.

She went to school the next day, and then she came home to her room. She did not mark the calendar with her pencil. She didn't mark it on the day after that either, or the one after that. The calendar hung, the days unmarked.

On the fourth day she told her grandmother she was sick. She couldn't go to school.

She lay in her bed. It was white and cool. No breeze stirred. She slept. She went, in a dream, with a friend on a journey through a long, long night, in a car that traveled fast, without stopping at all. Through blinking towns the car went, through the small hours of the night. It crossed a dark border in the dead, dark night. And they were smuggled—fugitives—by people they'd never met, and they were fed, and housed, and they whispered, and whispered, and then a train, and then a plane, and they still sped on. And then she woke up. She saw the white room and a pale shadow now, from the net curtain. And she continued the dream, because she remembered that he (but not she) had a mission, a very, very important mission. He would be for many months an exile under a wide sky, with a gun burning hot from the sun. The sun that bleached everything away, so that all that was left was what he had to do.

She lay for two days in her room, in the blinding sun. She did not sleep.

And then she went back to school. But she never marked the calendar again, not for one of the twenty-six days that remained, and her grandmother kept asking her, what's the matter, what's the matter, because she was very pale and she wasn't eating very much and because the calendar hung abandoned and the pencil too.

And it was on a day in December of 1977, as scheduled, that she boarded a plane bound for London's Heathrow. Her grandmother watched her walking through the glass doors, away, and said that she never looked back.

She often thought she would like to have told him about what she saw, where she went. She would like to have told him about the plays by Shakespeare that she saw, because she knows he would have enjoyed them. And she would like to have told him about the other interesting and important things that she saw, because she knows he would have enjoyed them. They were all the interesting and important things that she expected to see. But she would like to have told him that nothing she saw was as interesting, or as important, as what she left behind.

The Letter

I T ·WAS IN THE DAYS when I worked at the hotel. I had a
partner. Rose was my partner. Our shift started at eight,
and I had to leave the house at six. In the winter months
it was still dark. I liked it because it was quiet still in the morning,
the children sleeping. There were a lot of us in the house those
days. My husband was in Diepkloof at the mine hostel. I had the
four children, my mother, my sister-in-law, her three children.
All in the two rooms. That's how it was.

But it was a good job I had in the hotel. It was regular, the pay
was better than before, how it was in Athol. And no boss lady to
fight with. You know. So I used to get up, drink my tea, and go.
I could smell the coalfires from the night before and I needed my
cardigan, even in summer, because of the early morning cold. I
would hurry along the path to my first bus. There'd be a line
already, a long line. In those days the buses were very bad.
Sometimes the bus didn't come at all, and then I would walk to
the station for Orlando West. The second bus was even more

crowded. I was happy when I got to Rissik Street, and the sun was coming up now, and I could see the hotel—stretching up to the sky in front of me. It's a skyscraper: you know it. Johannesburg's first five-star hotel. That's what they said.

I think Rose had the same journey to get to work as I did because she also lived in Soweto. But I never saw her, not on the first bus, not at the bus station, and not on the second bus. Not even on the walk along Rissik Street. I used to look for her. There were many commuters, I suppose that's why I didn't see her. Walking, everyone walking, going into Jo'burg to work.

Rose had only her boy at home. We used to joke about that. Because I was always complaining about my sister-in-law and her children in our house. My sister-in-law's husband was working those days in Pietersburg. What a racket there was in the house, and my sister-in-law cheeky and getting on my nerves. Oh, she got on my nerves, all right. Lucky she moved out a few years after that, when she found that other man. But in the meantime I had to manage with her. You know how it was. But Rose at her house, there was just her and her boy. He was twelve years old the time I met Rose. That was in 1972, I remember, because that was the year I got the job in the hotel.

Rose told me her husband had long gone, and good riddance. That's what she said: good riddance. She said he was no good. She said he was lazy, no job ever, and drinking a lot. She told me he threw a bottle one time inside the house, and shouting, shouting. After all the broken glass, and then the boy crying, he went out, slamming the door something terrible. The whole house shook, she told me. And cursing and cursing something terrible. And he never came back again.

So she had a hard job on her own, raising the boy. Bringing him up on her own. But the boy was completely different from his father. Thanks to God about that, Rose said. Thanks to God. He looks like his father, she said, same dark colour. And same tall and thin. But other than that, it's night and day. So Rose said. Night and day. Her boy was a good boy. A serious boy. And good in school! Rose was so proud of that. When the report card came home, oh, Rose used to tell me all the marks. A+ in arithmetic, A+ in English, even A+ in Afrikaans, that nobody wants to learn. My children didn't get many report cards. You remember how it was. Even with my mother in the house, and my sister-in-law, the children didn't go so much to school. My sister-in-law, she pays no attention to children and school. She is busy talking, talking. Always talking. And worrying about some man that she saw at the Indian's shop on the corner. No-good ones also. You know how they hang around there. Just hang around doing nothing. And she always got trouble with jobs. Doesn't like this job, doesn't like that job. So her children mostly running, running in the path back there, no shoes, nothing. My children mostly the same, with no one properly to watch. It pains me to say it, but it's true. That's how it was.

But Rose's boy was different. Rose always worried about him. She worried that he should have shoes for school. A boy must have shoes for school, she said. To show he's serious. That's what she said. And him growing so fast, Rose was always buying him shoes. She found a shop on Rissik Street. I think the man gave her a good bargain on the black school shoes, because he saw her coming every six months, worried and worried about the shoes.

And another thing, the boy went to church with Rose on Sundays. My children, you can't make them darken that door of church on Sundays—never. But Rose's boy came. He would sit with her in the benches, listening to the priest. All what the priest said, he listened. Rose also listened I think to everything that priest said. Me—I don't listen so much to what the white priest says. Because what does he know. You know? What does he know? And telling us always to be good, to be godly, then good will come. I stopped believing him long time ago. But I think Rose believed him. That's why Rose always cleaning, sweeping her house also. She told me when she comes home from work she starts sweeping up, cleaning up. And ironing the boy's school shirts. I would be thinking of her doing that. When I was at home with the racket and my sister-in-law arguing with everyone, I would think of Rose in her house, sweeping up everything for her boy, setting out his bread for the morning when she would be long gone to the hotel. She heard that priest say cleanliness is next to godliness (because I heard him say that once). But I don't believe that. I don't see much godliness, so I don't believe him any more, that priest. But that was me, and Rose was Rose.

So Rose was always telling me the boy's going to finish his schooling. He's going to be a school teacher one day. I was happy for her. I was happy because we need more school teachers in Soweto. Of course. So I was happy about that, and I was happy to hear about the boy.

In the meantime, Rose and I started work at eight each day. We'd change into our uniforms in the basement laundry of the hotel. The uniform was dark blue, and it said "Carlton Hotel" in white letters on the shoulder. We looked smart. It was quite a hotel. You've seen it, up in the sky there: it's got thirty floors. A five-star hotel. Oh, they were always telling us that, at the hotel. Five-star this, five-star that. Service this, service that.

Me and Rose had four floors of rooms to clean every day, and the other teams got other floors. We had a routine. Rose would do the bathrooms, while I did the beds and vacuumed. Then we would switch. We were good together. We never had an argument. We kept far away from the head housekeeper, and from the other white people in charge: the receptionists, the restaurant manager. That was Rose's idea. Stay out of trouble, that's what she said. We had to deliver the tablecloths to the restaurant in the mornings. We'd see the tables and all the glasses stacked. Our boss, Josephine, was from Soweto also, so if we needed anything—

more towels for room 310, an extra blanket for room 209, one time a new mattress for the penthouse—we'd ask Josephine. It was no problem. No arguing with a boss who wanted this, wanted that. Rose had that before, she told me, when she was a domestic in Athol. With the boss ladies in the big houses, so fussy, so fussy. Now we didn't have those problems any more.

We laughed a lot also at work those days, me and Rose. We'd see things in the rooms. There were businessmen from Cape Town who had women, you know, sent up by the porters at night. Fancy ones with long, shiny legs and long yellow hair. Rose and me saw them those days. There were German tourists one time, with their cameras and their language that sounds like Afrikaans. I heard they were like the Afrikaners too, those Germans, but I never saw for myself. They gave good tips, so that was fine with me. One of them left twenty rand for the maids on the table. Me and Rose planned all afternoon what we'd do with twenty rand extra. I joked with Rose it was an advance on her boy's next pair of shoes. She laughed at that, but God's truth, that's what it was, I'm thinking now.

When Rose's boy was nearing matriculation, that was in 1976, there was all the big trouble with the schools: the protests every day, and the police in the streets. Rose told me he still went to school, even though the schools weren't open so much, but he still went, and he did his homework, and his teacher sent special work home with him. He sent work home special with Rose's boy, because Rose's boy was so good and wanting to learn. But I think Rose was getting worried in those days, about the school, and about matriculation. I was worried also because of the trouble in the streets, and the police in the streets. So I told my children and my sister-in-law, stay in the house, see, stay in the house. So mostly those days I think they were staying in the house, or they were running on the path behind, but not on the streets any more. That's how it was.

One day Rose didn't come to work. It was the first time that happened. Rose was always at work. Even if Rose had a cold and was coughing all over the place, she came to work. I told Josephine I think it's the boy must have trouble, otherwise Rose would surely be at work. I had to get another partner for work that day. It wasn't nearly so good either, with the partner I got that day.

When Rose came to work the next day she told me she can't talk loud any more. I said what you mean you can't talk loud. Rose says we have to be speaking careful now. Rose didn't have her usual carefree way. You know? It took her a long time to explain it to me, because I think she was not understanding so well herself what was going on. And me, I'm not understanding so well either. Because I never had anything to do with all that before. I never knew what's going on with the political people. And we were afraid, you know. So Rose told me her boy had been going to a house at night sometimes, where there were the political people, talking, talking. The boy didn't pay so much attention to his homework any more, she said. She found out by accident, that's what bothered her a lot also. He said he was going to do his homework with a friend, and one night she followed him a way up the back street, and she saw the house, and the boys who were going in there. She knew about that kind of house. They talk and talk in the night in those houses. They smoke cigarettes. They do work for the leaders on the Island. I don't know. We keep away from those houses because we don't want trouble with the police. You know how it is. But that's where Rose's boy was in the evenings now.

Rose told me she shouted at the boy. No, it's no good, she said. You'll end up on the Island too, she told him. She cried and cried. That's what she told me. She was shaking and afraid in her house now. And her boy, he takes his books to the paraffin lamp and he reads and does his homework still, but Rose thinks there's other books he reads now also. Books from the other house where he goes. Rose isn't sure now. But Rose was very afraid also to talk.

So for a few months Rose was agitated at work, and she was afraid of talking, but she would still be talking. I would listen, then I would try to tell her her boy is clever, he's a clever boy, he won't do something stupid. And I told her maybe something good would come out of it, because all the other clever ones are on the Island but they say they will change things one day. I don't know. I don't know. It was a long time then the leaders were on the Island, and nothing come of all that. Rose was very upset. I used to come home upset also. I felt very nervous, in truth. Because then I got to thinking if the police find Rose's boy and what he's doing, then they will find Rose, and if they find Rose they will find me, because I work in the hotel with Rose. I wasn't sure what the police could want with me, but you never know. You have to keep away from them. They want to know things always about people who are making plans. They don't want plans. That's how it is.

My sister-in-law meantime was just carrying on as usual with a new man she found at the Indian's shop, another no-good one, and he used to come and hang around at night in my house, and drink meths in front of the children, and keep the children up. I was getting very upset with everything in those days, because then in the mornings I had to go to work and see Rose who was also getting more and more agitated.

Then one terrible day Rose came to work, but as soon as I saw her in the laundry by the uniforms I knew it was a very bad day. She was shaking when she took her uniform. That day Rose sat mostly on the beds in all the rooms we were cleaning and cried many tears. I did all the work, and I was sweating because I wanted to cover for Rose, but I was also sweating because of what she told me. Her boy had left the night before, in the middle of the night. He was gone to Lusaka, in Zambia, up there, gone. Gone,

I said. What you mean gone. He told Rose the Movement was sending him away to the training camp overseas. It had all been long planned, but he couldn't tell Rose before because it was very dangerous. She must not know. That's another reason I was sweating: because now I knew about this boy who had been sent by the Movement to train overseas. To train and come back with guns and bombs and everything. Rose kept saying, guns and bombs and guns and bombs and everything and then she would be crying again. He's only seventeen years old Rose said, many times. Many times she said that. And I would be thinking about the black school shoes, and the report card with a line of A+'s all the way down, and my heart was deep sore too.

And of course I couldn't tell anybody all this. Not my mother at home, not my sister-in-law—definitely not her—not even my husband at Diepkloof who came once a month. So every night at home I would go to bed and be worrying about Rose and her boy. And every morning I would see Rose at the pile of laundry, and no sooner were we safe in one of the rooms, cleaning, and she would start up again about Lusaka, but whispering, so whispering. How frightened we were.

But Rose got herself calmed down soon after that. She was tough. She told me she was going to wait, because he would come back, and what he said would come true. There would be a new government, and new laws. Then everything would be better, because of what they were doing in Lusaka. He was a clever boy, of course. He wouldn't do something foolish. He could see that there was no use going to school in Soweto, it would come to nothing. It had never come to anything, going to school in Soweto. The schools in Soweto were rubbish in any case, that's what he said to Rose.

So Rose was a bit better. But another other thing her boy had told her was, he would write to her, when he could. This turned out to be a big mistake, to tell her that. Because after about two months of him being away, she started on about the letter. How come she didn't have a letter yet.

She told me that one day a letter would come to her mailbox. Yes Rose, I told her, yes, he said he would send a letter. Not the brown envelope with the square black writing, addressed to "The Occupant," from the City of Johannesburg, Municipal Services, that came every month reminding her to pay her rent. No, a real letter, with her name written on it, in a careful, rounded print. That's what she said. Even I could imagine the letter then. A little grimy, the letter would be, because it would have come from very far away. It would have a stamp on it we'd never seen. Maybe the stamp would be coloured, with a picture of another place, far away. There would be no return address on the back. Rose would sit down with the letter, hold it in her hands. And I would imagine that, too.

And many times, when we were cleaning the rooms, Rose told me about the long, long journey that letter would travel to reach her. She would describe the journey of the letter, and I would listen. The letter would be folded carefully by the hands of her son. Hands rough and calloused, not smooth as a schoolboy's, any more. The letter, Rose said, would pass from his hands to another hand, and to another. It would go into a cardboard box, and then into a wooden one. It would travel on a lorry that hurtled along a road across a wide, grassy plain. It would arrive in a bustling African city, filled with people, many people. It would travel to an airport. And then, if the letter had not fallen out of the cardboard box, or the wooden box, or the lorry; if it had not fallen from one of the pairs of hands that had passed it here, and passed it there; then an airplane would carry the letter in its cargo, and surely a letter cannot fall out of an airplane, and into the blank, blue sky?

And Rose said that the airplane would fly south, almost as far south as airplanes fly. And she had to trust that in Johannesburg, where it would arrive, they take care of letters that have come from far away, and watch that they don't fall out of boxes and crates and bags and people's hands, and Rose knew the Johannesburg Central Post Office because she saw it on her way to work every morning, and it was a building that was made of bricks not prefab and it looked very solid indeed and it looked as if it would be very good at taking care of letters and especially letters from very very far away. And I knew that post office because I saw it every morning also, so I knew just what Rose meant.

And one day—Rose said—the mailman whose area was Orlando West would deliver the letter into the mailbox of house number 1665. Rose's mailbox. Rose's house. And I would imagine that, too.

But many months went by, and no letter came. We carried on with our work, day after day, at the hotel. One day I told Rose maybe her mailbox is not the right place for a letter to be delivered from the Resistance far, far away. Maybe the letter would come by a different route. A secret route. Maybe it would be smuggled in, by people who cross borders against the law, and cross out again, in the night. A letter much creased and folded, such a letter would be. It would be delivered by a person Rose would never meet, and never see. She would find such a letter pushed under her door one morning when she set out for work. Who knows? That's what I said to Rose.

But it was a terrible mistake to tell Rose this. Because then Rose became very anxious about sounds outside her house at night. That's what she told me. She was certain that a person from the Resistance was waiting always in the shadows to deliver a letter to her. And I became very nervous too, even in my own house at night. Because I started to think that the person from the Resistance was waiting to communicate with me, too. To help Rose. Because I was Rose's friend. And then I couldn't sleep at night at all, for many months.

And at night, when I was lying in my bed, I would imagine this letter that did not come. I imagined that whichever way this letter would come, Rose would open the letter, as she sat at her table. She would flatten the creases. And she would read. I am well, mother, I am well. We will succeed, mother, we will succeed in our struggle. Have faith and be patient, mother. Be patient. That's what I used to imagine, when I lay in my bed at night.

But Rose told me one day that she was thinking something else. Something much worse by far. Maybe no letter would come. No letter ever. Instead—she said—there would be a knock on her door one quiet, far-off night. A young man would stand in her doorway. He would have a heavy step, this young man, and a heavier heart. He would deliver news; news that no mother can bear.

Rose left her job soon after she told me that. She couldn't work any more. She couldn't concentrate, she did everything wrong, and then she got in trouble because she forgot all the towels for the rooms one day. She wanted to be at home to wait for the letter, she told me. She must wait at home. That's what she told me. I got a new partner at the hotel. I didn't enjoy it so much, ever again, working in that hotel, and one day the next year I got another job altogether.

I went to visit Rose once after that, at her house in Orlando. But her sister was looking after her that time, even paying her rent, and cooking for her, otherwise Rose wouldn't eat. That's what her sister told me. She told me Rose stays in the house all day, and waits for her boy. She told me Rose is waiting for a letter still. Now Rose says the letter will come from Dar es Salaam. All the way from Dar, that's what they call it. That's where she heard some of those boys are now. And if a letter does not come from Dar es Salaam, then a young man—a comrade—will come to Rose's door. And Rose must be home to meet this young man. That's what Rose told me. .

And while I was sitting in a chair with my tea, in Rose's house, Rose told me she travels every day across a wide, grassy plain in a lorry that hurtles, to a bustling city. It's called Lusaka, Rose told me. And then she flies in an airplane through the blue, blue sky, where it's so beautiful, she said. She flies like a bird, south, south, as far south as airplanes fly. Because she is a letter, she told me, that must, must be delivered to a mailbox in Orlando West, in the Republic of South Africa. This mailbox, which is number 1665, stands in a very, very dark place that is far away from all help. And help is needed, Rose told me. Help is needed. That's what Rose told me that day.

Freedom Fighter

H E'S WAITING AT THE CORNER of the dirt road. It's night. He hears a distant dog bark; some laughter nearby. He stands in the shadows. He himself is a shadow, wavering. There is the smell of coalfires, that is the smell of his home. He breathes it in. He's a living, breathing shadow.

He carries nothing. That was his instruction. He wears a sweater, although it's warm out. He is aware of his heart beating, just a little faster than normal. His breathing too is faster, shallower than normal. He tries to slow his breathing, to deepen it. He's waiting for the car. It's late, the car. The minutes crawl by.

He's picturing the car that will pick him up. It will speed through the night, on long, silent roads, through blinking towns. It will not stop at all, not for nothing will it stop. Not at any single town, in the live, live night. Not at any petrol station, either, at no house, at no crossing. It will pass police stations in small country towns, at quiet crossroads. Manned inside; always manned. But the car will not stop. It will speed on, on. It will arrive at a distant, scrubby border in the deepest dark. It will cross the border, in the silence. There will be the sound of the car's engine. And that is all.

And he's picturing the train he will take then, and many more hours. There will be people that he will meet, and houses to shelter him. He will truly be a shadow. A fugitive fleeing his country.

And he will arrive—at last—in the distant country where his comrades are. There will be flashing smiles, the talk in his language, jubilant handshakes: the triumph of his arrival in the strange place. And his work will begin.

He is picturing that work, and he's had a dream for some months now, about that work. He's replaying the dream in his mind. It is what sustains him as he waits for the car at the dark, still corner. It's like a tape that he runs in his mind.

It goes like this. He's in the sky. The sky is a vast, pale blue. It stretches as far as the eye can see. There's a sun, too. It is always there. He is in the sky, and he's looking down on a dun landscape. It is a plain, this landscape, a vast flat plain. It lies below him, spread out. He can move over the land. He can watch it, as he glides.

And he sees the land dotted at far intervals with installations, instalations that he has studied and knows. The bridge over there. It spans the great brown river, the river that wends its way to the sea. He follows the river with his eyes, he follows its wide curves. And there's the dam, the dam that harnesses the power. He knows its shape, that dam, how it curves. He follows its curve. He knows what the engineers did, when they built it, the principles they applied. He knows the dam's secrets.

And he travels on. There's land, more land. He wheels and turns. And he sees it: the mine. It unspools into view. It is a black labyrinth—a spider, many-tentacled—on the brown land. He knows everything about that mine. How it's laid out, how deep it goes. Where its shafts are. He knows the angles of the shafts.

And he sees the road; the road that leads to the mine. It's an artery. Essential. He sees the other roads, arterial. He follows them. He can follow them blindfold. He follows them to gates.

He nods at the gatekeeper, hard-hatted in his chair. He passes through the gates, passes. He's done this many times. Each time his heart almost stops in his chest.

And now he follows the mine shafts—down, down, in his mind. He goes very deep down the shafts. It is dark and cool. He would rest there. But then it's burning hot; he's engulfed in heat, as from an oven. It's heat that kills. The miners, he sees their glistening faces. He hears their breathing, laboured. He sees their progress: slow, and perilous. He will ascend. He ascends and emerges into bright light, blinking.

He's in the sky again. He turns, looks down. He watches the miners streaming out of the gates. He has watched them many times. Streaming out of the gates, like ants. And so he knows when the shafts are empty. He knows how to wait.

He moves on, closer now to the sun. He looks down, the earth spread below. He sees all that he knows.

And he knows all this—all the roads and gates, the shafts and towers, the dams and bridges—because he will have studied them on maps from far away. From the faraway country where his comrades are, he will study this landscape. There are maps and diagrams in detail. White papers and charts, unrolled and unfurled, corners held down with stones. They are traced with lines of black: razor-thin. And arrows. And one arrow: red. Pinpoints of precision. He will sit under a wide sky, under trees that don't shade, and he will study those maps. With his comrades, intent. He was always a good student, and he's a good student now. He will know perfectly what he needs to know. He will know every thing.

He looks down now in his dream. His eagle eye (and he is an eagle, after all, in the dream) finds just what he's looking for. It's the power station. It sprawls. It glints silver. Just a little. It's a taunt.

He holds the power station glinting in his sights. He holds it. He holds its life in his hands (in his eyes). He has immense power.

The dream ends. The tape runs out. The darkness drops.

The car—late—comes at last. Its engine purrs. Its headlights pick out the stones in the road, in circular pools. He gets in. The door slams. The car drives away.

The street corner is empty. There's just the moon: a witness. He's a boy who's left home. He's seventeen years old.

Acknowledgements

To Olive Senior and M G Vassanji, who made this a better book.
To Antanas Sileika, who guided me crucially.
To Amatoritsero Ede, who published my first story.
To Nurjehan Aziz, who puts stories into the world, where they belong.
To Peggy Stockdale, talented designer.
To Helen Walsh, Nalo Hopkinson, and Diaspora Dialogues.
To the Humber School for Writers.
To the Ontario Arts Council for generous financial assistance.
To my husband and two children, who are with me every single day.